W9-BNN-482

River of Gold

Donald Willerton

Terra Nova Books
SANTA FE, NEW MEXICO

Library of Congress Control Number 2018951006

Distributed by SCB Distributors, (800) 729-6423

Terra Nova Books

River of Gold © 2018 by Donald Willerton
All rights reserved
Published 2018
Printed in the United States of America

The characters and many of the events in this book are fictional, and any
similarity to actual events or people is coincidental.

Published by Terra Nova Books, Santa Fe, New Mexico.
www.TerraNovaBooks.com

ISBN 978-1-948749-02-2

For My Mother

CHAPTER

1

Chama, New Mexico Territory, October 1881

"Everett, we gotta find us a way to get big money. This slave work is about to kill me!"

Orin and Everett Cossey had come back from the grub shack and were sitting next to a small stream. It had been a long day, and the brothers had only an hour before dark. After another typically restless night in the crowded crew tents, morning would find them back at the rough and tough job of laying railroad track.

"Well, Orin, I just don't see how to work much harder, and it don't seem like they's goin' to pay us more, so we are stuck with what we are doin', I think."

Back in the spring, the Denver and Rio Grande Railroad had finished laying tracks over the Colorado mountains and into a sleepy little village in the New Mexico Territory called Chama. With the tracks complete to the middle of town, the track boss switched some of the crews to building a locomotive roundhouse, a repair shop, dormitories, and a depot building while others built a sawmill to cut the lumber needed for the construction. That took the rest of the summer.

Now in the fall, as the air chilled and the aspen leaves yellowed, the boss put them back to making roadbed and laying rails straight west out of Chama toward Lumberton. When the snows came, he'd put the crews into camps for the winter, downing every tree they saw to make the heavy wooden ties needed to support the rails. The D&RG wanted to be at the mines in Silverton by the end of the following year, and they'd need thousands of ties to make that deadline.

"There you go, tryin' to think again," Orin answered with his usual response to any comment from Everett. "That ain't the kind of money I'm talkin' about. I'm talkin' big money—BIG! We gots to get out of here, go do somethin' that will get us enough money so's we don't have to work for no bossman no more. I'm tired of havin' somebody tell me what to do when they's ain't workin' a lick."

It was this way every night, Everett listening to his big brother carry on about going someplace, about doing something, about making it big and not having to work. It had been that way ever since they'd left Arkansas— Lord, how many years had it been?

Orin's original plan was for them to go to Texas to become cattlemen. It ended with their working as drovers, choking on dust while driving herds of cattle north to Kansas. Then his plan changed to include cattle rustling on the side, one of those "big money" moves that got them nothing but a quick escape into Colorado.

Then his plan was to find bucketloads of silver up in Leadville. That plan ended after six months of freezing inside a granite mountain and a firm hand on their necks as the sheriff threw them out of town for printing up false mining claims.

What then? A month or so in Durango, then a spell in Dodge City, Kansas, where Orin tried his luck at gambling. That was supposed to be a "big money" move, too. And now they were humping railroad ties to the barking of a track boss in a damned wilderness.

"Ya know," Orin said casually as he threw rocks into the stream. "Every month, they's shippin' a strongbox of gold down to the bank in Tierra Amarilla. They's goin' to lay a spur down that ways, and when they do, that there deposit money will go by train, whereas they now takes it by wagon. If 'n somebody was goin' to steal one of them strongboxes, it'd be before next summer, 'cause after that, you'd have to stop a train rather than a wagon. A strongbox, I hear, holds a powerful lot of money."

Everett listened with only one ear. It didn't matter whether he heard everything or whether he agreed or not or whether he had any concerns. One way or another, Orin was going to come up with a plan—a plan where Orin would do whatever he wanted and Everett would have to do it with him. That's what Momma had said that he as the younger brother should do, though she hadn't thought it out, Everett realized. Momma expected Orin to take care of Everett but hadn't considered it might mean being hung on a gallows beside him.

* * *

The road to Tierra Amarilla, May 1882

It was May, and Everett Cossey was talking to himself. "We shouldn't be doin' this," he whispered under his breath. "This is a bad deal," he said. "Oh, Lord, Orin," he almost yelled out, "what would Momma be thinkin'?"

Sweat ran down his face as he fidgeted in the dirt. Kneeling behind a boulder, shifting from one knee to the other, trying to conceal himself completely—trying, in fact, to be invisible—he hoped that Orin would forget about him. He should never have gone along with it, should never have let Orin plan this thing, this horrible, horrible thing. They had done bad things in the past but had never outright killed anybody.

But Orin was in charge, Momma had told him. Always, it was Orin who would give the orders, always Orin who would decide things, always Orin who would tell Everett what to do.

But Momma couldn't have meant killing people. Never, ever.

An hour earlier, Orin had sent Tom back along the road to climb up a small hill. When the jail wagon came into view, he was to give a wave and run back. Luke was in the rocks below the road, ready to cut the rope holding the tree, and Jug was in the bushes on the left, ready to shoot anyone in the back of the wagon or inside the cage.

That left Everett in front of where the wagon would be stopped, with Orin behind him on his horse, hidden in the trees. Orin would ride out when the wagon heaved to, but he expected Everett and Jug to already be firing.

"As soon as the tree falls across the road, kill the driver and anybody with him," Orin had told them in no uncertain terms. "Don't wait for the dirt to settle. Kill them before they have a chance to shoulder their guns."

The Tierra Amarilla bank didn't have a real strongbox wagon, one of those fancy rigs that had a big iron box on wheels with a shotgun man inside who could shoot through the little windows. Instead, the bank used the sheriff's jail wagon, which wasn't much for protecting things—just a cage of iron bars set on a wagon frame where the sheriff kept the prisoners he collected as he rode among the villages and outposts around the backcountry. The bank thought the strongbox inside the iron cage was secure enough, not so much because it was well protected but because no bandit would be stupid enough to rob the wagon as it moved the strongbox from the train in Chama down the road to Tierra Amarilla. It wasn't much more than thirteen miles between the two towns, and there wouldn't be enough time for anybody to rob the wagon and get away before the sheriff would be after them. A bandit would be crazy to attempt it.

Which was all part of Orin Cossey's plan.

Tom's hand shot into the air. Orin pulled the reins tight, making his horse stamp the ground all nervous like, and Everett could see Luke's eyes getting big, staring at Orin between glimpses at the dust in the distance.

When the bank wagon got within thirty yards, Orin pointed at Luke, Luke cut the rope, the tree fell across the road, the wagon driver yanked back on the reins, the horses reared, and the guard blasted Luke with his shotgun before Orin put two slugs into his chest. With no one in the back of the wagon, Jug shot the driver.

Everett had stood up behind the rock but did not fire. By the time his hand stopped shaking enough to hold his pistol steady, there was no one left to kill.

"Get that wagon off the road," Orin yelled at him, "since you ain't got guts 'nough to kill when killin' is needed!"

Everett obeyed.

The tree was dragged from the road, the wagon driven into the woods, and the tracks brushed out. The cage lock was shot off, the strongbox thrown to the ground and broken open, and the bags of gold coins moved to saddlebags. The dead bodies, including Luke's, were thrown into the cage.

Once the saddlebags were tied behind the four saddles, Orin spurred his horse north, and Everett spurred his southwest. Tom dropped into an arroyo to the left. Jug followed Orin, then Tom, and then went off on his own. Creating a maze of tracks in the grass, dirt, and sagebrush, each circled back to a cow trail that skirted the nearby Rio Chama flowing south. They rode together, urging their horses on, hot and panicked, trying not to think of what they had done.

Within an hour from when the wagon was stopped, they passed out of sight to the west of Tierra Amarilla.

When the gold wagon was late, the bank manager nervously paced in his office, but the sheriff was unconcerned. Delays were common in this rough country— there could be fallen rocks on the road, or maybe a washout. It was an hour more before the sheriff finally rode out of town.

By that time, the four outlaws had reached the Rio Cebolla, a small stream running out of the mountains east of the valley. They turned and headed west, following the stream. But when Orin and his outlaw band reached where the Cebolla ran into the Chama, Orin's carefully thought-out plan suddenly ran into problems.

The first problem was that the river was flooding.

Orin and Everett had scouted the river crossing in late February but had not understood how much the river would change when the snow in the mountains melted. Now that it was spring, the water cascading down from the high valleys had swelled the Rio Chama to four or five times the amount of water it held in late winter. Sitting on their horses next to a high bank, the Cossey brothers were looking at a thundering torrent of swirling water racing down the riverbed, maybe two feet higher than what they had seen before and a great deal more vicious.

Orin was stunned, then angry, then furious, drawing his pistol and shooting several times into the water as if to punish it for daring to go against his plan.

The second problem involved the small homemade boat they had bought from a rancher, and which he and Everett had hidden along the banks of the river. It was the key to the whole robbery.

Orin had intended to put the bags of gold into the boat and then row the boat into the deepest part of the Rio Chama canyon, a canyon so steep and narrow that no posse would imagine any outlaw venturing there. The bandits would bury the gold in the canyon and return for it later. It would never occur to the sheriff that the gold was in the canyon, so it would never be looked for. And if any of the thieves were caught later on, they could claim innocence as they would have no evidence of the robbery in their possession.

According to the plan, the man who would retrieve the boat from its hiding place and load the bags of coins into it, the man who would take the boat down the river and bury the gold, the man who was now struggling to control the overburdened boat in the bumping, swaying, lurching current, was Everett.

Arguing with Orin, pointing out the impossibility of piloting or even managing the boat in the swirling torrent, reminding him of the danger of high water in a low boat, pointing to the size of the waves, Everett did everything to change the plan except refuse.

Orin paid him no attention.

As his brother protested, panicking as he sat on the thin board that made the boat's seat, Orin cut the rope holding the boat to the bank. It was immediately swept into the surging water with Everett clinging helplessly to its sides, ignoring the paddle, talking a blue streak that soon grew into a series of screams. The small boat bucked and swirled and twisted in the angry water. Less than a minute later, it was out of sight in the dark shadows of the narrow canyon.

Orin had drawn a map of the canyon rim and river in February. At a place they had located, Everett would bury the gold and then wipe away any traces. At the other end of the deep canyon, not more than five or six miles away from the Rio Cebolla junction, where the tall sandstone walls spread out into a wide plain, Orin would be waiting for him, having ridden up into the mesas and doubled back to the river to lose the posse that would probably be on his tail.

After sinking the boat by bashing a hole in the bottom, the two brothers would race to the plateaus west of the small Spanish village of Abiquiu, twenty miles away. They would follow old Indian trails and disappear into the mountains while the other gang members would ride north for Colorado.

In exactly four months, long after the law had abandoned its pursuit, the bandits would meet up on the Rio

Chama where the river comes out of the narrow canyon. Orin would dig up the gold and divide it equally. Each of them would be rich for the rest of their lives.

That was the plan.

As Everett and the boat disappeared into the canyon's darkness, Orin and the other two men put spurs to their horses, fought the ferocious current, and were soon galloping up the far trail. Once on high ground, they separated, each heading miles away to find fresh horses and supplies. Changing mounts and chasing their used horses in different directions, the outlaws raced away as if the devil himself was after them.

CHAPTER

Present Day

"I hear you two know your way around rafts." The voice was soft and had a strong Southern drawl.

"Yes sir, that's true," Mogi Franklin answered as his sister, Jennifer, stepped out of the garden and joined them. "We've both run rafts on the San Juan in Utah, working for San Juan River Expeditions in Mexican Hat."

"Well, it would mean getting out of the pumpkin patch for two or three days, but we could use your services if you're interested." The man was dressed in well worn but clean jeans, a summer work shirt, work boots, and a broad cowboy hat. He had a friendly, easy smile.

"That'd be great!" Mogi responded. He loved any excuse to get out of "the patch"—nearly an acre of carefully tended vegetables, melons, and herbs that provided most of the fresh produce used in the Ghost Ranch kitchen.

Jennifer was not disappointed either though she enjoyed working among the plants. She liked knowing that the aromatic tomatoes, onions, cantaloupes, and watermelons would make it to the tables of the Ghost Ranch eating halls.

Besides, working in the garden every morning was certainly better than sweating at any of the summer jobs they might have gotten in Bluff, their home town in Utah. The slickrock country around Bluff would be a lot hotter, a lot drier, and the work even less interesting than picking lettuce.

Ghost Ranch was a retreat center owned by the Presbyterian Church. Many years earlier, it had been a private "dude ranch" in the middle of the wild, untouched lands of northern New Mexico. Located on a high plateau about seventy miles north of Santa Fe, it was a secret vacation spot for the rich and famous in the 1920s, '30s and '40s. When it was sold in the '50s, the facility was built up to include a conference center, a swimming pool, a large dining facility, two museums, and several groups of cabins, casitas, and apartments. It now offered educational and retreat programs for the general public.

Mogi, Jennifer, and their mom had driven down from Bluff on Sunday. Mrs. Franklin was teaching a writing seminar for three weeks at the ranch and had worked out an arrangement for her children to help out around the ranch for free room and board. Mogi appreciated the garden as it was related to food, but bending over all the time was not his favorite position.

At fourteen, Mogi was tall for his age, but his muscles had not yet caught up with his bones, so he was gangly and spindly and a little bit awkward, which is to say, normal for his position in life. He took after his mom's side of the family in his looks and shyness, but seemed to be a sum of both families on the brain side. He was smarter than most people around him—quick-minded, mentally disciplined, and orderly—and had a natural talent for solving puzzles.

Jennifer, who was three years older, definitely took after their father. Shorter than her brother by a half-foot, with thick, brown hair cut short, she was strong, athletic, and physically graceful; she also had a keen sense of human nature and loved being around people. Whereas Mogi was the obsessive, analytical, adventurous problem-solver, Jennifer was the cautious, emotionally centered people person. He pushed her to do more than she thought she ought to; she pulled him back into what was reasonable.

"Well, wash your hands and come walk with me to the maintenance shed," the man said. "We'll see if our rafts still hold air."

Ted Allen was the go-to guy for anything and everything mechanical at the ranch, from the faucets in the guesthouses to the engine on the road grader; he also attended to the guests' needs. When he introduced himself at a campfire talk one night, he shared that he'd grown up in South Texas on a ranch, learned to handle cattle and horses as a young boy, earned a science degree, and then served in the Peace Corps for three years. He had jumped at the chance to work at Ghost Ranch ten years earlier and was still happy to be there every day.

"We used to offer raft trips as one of the regular outings for guests," Ted explained as the three walked toward a maintenance building. "But overnight trips got kind of expensive, and we let it go."

Ted pulled back one of the large sliding doors and led Mogi and Jennifer inside.

"We've got three rafts," he said as he led them to a corner of the shed, moved aside a pile of fencing material, and revealed a shelf holding what Mogi recognized as folded rafts.

"What river are you talking about?" Jennifer asked.

"The Rio Chama, on the other side of the valley. We get on the river right below El Vado Dam, west of Tierra Amarilla, and we get off at a bend in the river called Big Eddy, about thirty miles later. The road to Big Eddy is just a few miles above Abiquiu Lake, so it's only a short drive to get back here once we're off the river."

It took the three of them thirty minutes to drag each bundle out to the concrete apron in front of the shed, undo the straps, and flatten out each raft, which were old and dusty.

Ted came out with a vacuum cleaner. Reversing the hose, they used the vacuum to blow air into the rafts and then a water hose to wash them off. They all seemed airtight.

Ted also showed the Franklins the frames, oars, life jackets, straps, and other equipment. After another hour of washing and rigging, the rafts were ready to use.

"Your mother hinted that you two might be interested," Ted said. "A handful of people in her class were looking to do something on the river this weekend, but I had to tell them that although we had the equipment, we no longer had anybody experienced enough to pilot the rafts. But if you two will help me out, we'll put together a nice overnight trip for them."

It was no contest. Working in the garden each morning was fine, but rafting on one of New Mexico's most scenic rivers was a clear winner.

"If we pack up everything this afternoon, we should be ready to leave early tomorrow morning," Ted said. "Let's go talk to the kitchen folks about getting meals together for the trip."

* * *

"This is great!" Mogi called over to his sister as he pulled on his oar to turn the raft into the current.

He was used to the muddy waters of the San Juan River, as well as the deep, hot canyons of southern Utah. The Rio Chama was entirely different: cold, relatively clear water; green, pasture-like grasses and flatlands; pine trees and gambel oak thickets; and tall canyon walls of sandstone colored in yellows, browns, and whites.

Jennifer loved it. She let the raft slowly rotate so she could see the landscape around her. Instead of the uniform starkness of Utah stone, this canyon felt fatter and richer, wrapped by a thick robe of colors instead of a single-color curtain.

It was Saturday. Ted was in the first raft, Jennifer in the second, and Mogi the third. Each had three attendees from the writing seminar as passengers. The day before, Ted had assembled the tents, sleeping bags, dry bags, food, drinking water, stove, table, cooking items, a makeshift toilet, and other gear needed for the overnight trip.

Now he called back to them, "Pull over around the next bend!"

Mogi slowed his raft as he watched Ted and Jennifer pull their rafts over to the right bank, next to the ruins of an old farmhouse. Angling to come in next to Jennifer, he soon tied up his raft and his passengers followed Ted up a short path.

"This is the Martinez homestead," Ted announced as he pointed toward the old leaning, two-story house, the tumbledown pig sheds, the bent wire fences, and a narrow, primitive road. "It was used by the Martinez family from the late 1800s until it was abandoned in the '50s. You're welcome to wander through the house and around the corrals."

It was tiny. Mogi couldn't believe that people lived in such small rooms. The kitchen was not much bigger than his closet at home. The floors were uneven, made of wide boards. The doorways were narrow and short while the ceilings were low enough for him to touch with his fingers. There was no inside stairway to the bedrooms of the second floor, only narrow stairs that went up the outside wall of the house.

"Look at this!" Jennifer called out. People gathered around. Where newspapers had been pasted over the walls to keep out the wind, she pointed to a yellowed article about a new baseball player named Babe Ruth and his latest game.

"Hey, look out here!" one of the guests called. He was outside, pointing at a small spring flowing from under the house, which pooled just before it ran into the river.

"It's a hot spring!" the man said laughing as he swirled his fingers in the bubbling water.

Pretty clever for keeping the house warm in winter, Mogi thought as he stepped over the small stream. Looking back to the rafts, he noticed the guest from California, Sheila Winters, kneeling next to Ted's raft.

Shiela was the guest who'd taken a full five minutes to introduce herself at the beginning of the raft trip. While the other guests were content to say their names, where they were from, and a few words about what they were enjoying about the writing seminar, Sheila went on and on until Ted finally interjected to end her tedious speech.

Mogi watched as she filled a small bottle with river water. She capped it off, dried the bottle against her leg, and used a marker to write something on its label. She placed the bottle into a canvas bag and dropped it into the raft. She had done the same thing when they were preparing the rafts to launch on the river.

Leaving the farmhouse behind, everyone returned to the rafts. After rowing for less than a minute, Ted brought them to the opposite bank and tied up.

"Everybody is wearing clothes that can get wet, right? We're going for a swim!"

The idea made several of the guests nervous; the water in the river was freezing cold, coming from the bottom of El Vado Lake, a reservoir held back by the dam.

Ted led them a hundred yards up the river to a flat piece of land that projected out from the bank. In the center of the flat ground was an almost circular body of water. He carefully stepped into the pool and sat down, the water rising up to his chest.

It was another hot spring, its circular shape and flat-rock bottom created over the years by visitors enjoying its waters. Mogi and Jennifer and the guests slowly lowered themselves into the pool with oohs and ahs and small squeals, settling around the rim. Sheila Winters had brought her canvas bag. After she lowered herself into the water, she pulled out an empty container, filled it with spring water, wrote on the outside, and placed it back in the bag.

She looked up with a guilty smile.

"I'm a biology teacher," she said. "I'll take these water samples back to my class where we'll test them with water quality kits and compare them with the water from around our own area. My students will love to hear that this water comes from a place called Ghost Ranch."

"Anyone know why Ghost Ranch is called Ghost Ranch?" Ted asked.

"I bet there's a ghost involved," a woman from Santa Fe said with a grin.

"Well, now, that's true, but there's a little more to the story," Ted began. "In the late 1880s, two brothers named Archuleta built a cabin at the mouth of a canyon on the Ghost Ranch property. The Archuletas were outlaws—cattle rustlers and thieves—and were using the dead-end canyon to hide herds of stolen cows.

"The local ranchers became suspicious when they never saw any herds during the day yet heard cattle being moved during the night. The situation got worse when some people new to the area passed through the ranch one night, hoping to find shelter. They were never seen again, but their belongings—saddles, bridles, and spurs—soon appeared on the Archuletas' horses. No one was brave enough to accuse them, but everyone assumed that the brothers had murdered the visitors and thrown their bodies down a dry well on the property.

"After that, shepherds grazing their sheep along the river next to the ranch began hearing mysterious sounds that they believed to be the wailings of those who had been murdered. They believed the ranch had become haunted and the whole area cursed. It was then referred to as *El Rancho de los Brujos*—The Ranch of the Witches.

"Time went by and the Archuleta brothers got into a squabble about money. One of them had hidden a jar full of money to keep the other from getting it, and one brother killed the other brother. That was more than the neighbors could stand, so a posse of local men went to the ranch and hung the second brother, plus everyone else who was working on the property. Well, their souls didn't stay quiet either, and the ranch was soon abandoned because of all the noisy ghosts flying around.

"The land changed hands a couple of times until 1928 when it was sold to a man named Salazar, who promptly lost the deed in a card game. The new owner gave the deed to his wife. Her name was Carol Bishop Stanley, and it is she who later moved to the ranch, renamed it Ghost Ranch, and started what was to become a well-respected getaway for rich vacationers from the East. That was the beginning of what you know as Ghost Ranch today."

Everyone clapped in appreciation.

"Any more stories?" one of the guests asked.

"As a matter of fact," Ted replied, "there's still the biggest and best known local mystery story, but I'll save it for tonight. It happened in the 1880s when two brothers robbed a pay wagon, killed everybody, made their escape, and hid the gold along the Rio Chama. You'll like it."

CHAPTER

3

"**N**o wonder Mom likes this country so much," Mogi said to Jennifer as they arranged their sleeping bags in the tent. "I've never seen colors like this."

The three rafts were tied up to a huge cottonwood tree along the riverbank at a well-used camping spot next to nearly vertical cliffs. As the sun went down, the colors of the canyon's towering sandstone columns—yellow, tan, red, and white—glowed in the softening light, contributing a richness to the atmosphere that combined the deep greens of the grasses and trees with the thick smell of the water to produce a soulful feeling as the rafters set up camp.

As the evening deepened, more shadows appeared on the walls, making the canyon around them seem more rugged and mysterious, even spooky, causing Mogi to remember the man he had seen in the forest that day.

It happened in mid-afternoon. There was a half-mile or so of flat land along the left bank where a smaller river from the east, called the Rio Cebolla, flowed into the Chama. It was a ribbon of water no more than four feet across when it met the main flow.

Just beyond where they joined, the Chama entered the deepest part of the canyon. Where the massive sandstone walls closed in on the riverbed, the canyon became noticeably narrower and darker as the sunlight no longer reached the river. It was both comforting and confining at the same time.

The three rafts had slowed in the flat water next to the Rio Cebolla but then sped up as the river entered the narrow gorge. A mile or so later, as Mogi steered his raft to enter a rapid, he glanced into the trees on the left side and saw a man standing in the shadows. The man stood quietly, as if content to simply watch the boaters go by. Not unusual, Mogi guessed, but the man wore no shirt, and his white skin looked odd against the background of trees and shadows. He was too far away to clearly see his face.

Mogi turned his attention to the raft as it swept through the rapid, and when he glanced back, the man was gone. It puzzled him.

"How was the food?" Ted asked the guests as they finished their supper and gathered around the campfire. He had used a large cast iron skillet to cook meat and vegetables that, when forked onto small flour tortillas and covered in cheese, tomatoes, and salsa, made delicious handheld *fajitas*. Everyone was appreciative and complimented him as they sat on blankets and in camp chairs.

"I promised you a mystery story of robbery and murder," Ted said. "It has the typical dead bodies, lost gold, and a ghost, but I would pay particular attention because it was right here, right in this area of the canyon, that the darkest part of the mystery took place. And, of course, you might keep an eye out for the ghost that's still flying around."

People smiled and looked at each other with anticipation. Mogi's expression grew more thoughtful.

"In 1882," Ted began, "monthly shipments of gold were made from a bank in Denver to a bank in Tierra Amarilla, that little town we passed through this morning on the way to the put-in at the bottom of the dam. The gold shipments were sent by rail from Denver to Chama, but at Chama, the railroad turned and went west to Durango, so the gold was loaded into a strongbox and taken the rest of the way by wagon.

"On May 19, five bandits hijacked the wagon, killed the driver and the guard, broke open the box, and stole several bags of gold coins, more than a hundred and fifty pounds worth. The bandits put the gold in their saddlebags and rode off. Remember that wide spot we passed on the left where a little stream joins the Chama? That's the Rio Cebolla. Well, the bandits came all the way down here to cross the Chama at that point.

"The bandits crossed the river and rode into the hills to the west. But when the sheriff's posse got to the crossing, they were less than enthusiastic about crossing the river because, it being May, the river was at flood stage. All the snow melting in the high country had swollen the river to three or four times its normal volume, which made it a big, roaring, dangerous torrent with very strong currents.

"Crossing a river like that on a horse was something you did only if you had to. Half of the men in the posse were afraid to risk it, so they turned back. Only the sheriff and two others crossed over and continued to chase the bandits, who were hours ahead of them.

"The bandits, meanwhile, once across the river, took every opportunity to cover their tracks by backtracking along the route and then changing to fresh horses that they had hidden in advance. It took the sheriff until late the next day to find a good set of horse tracks to follow.

"The sheriff and his deputies tracked three men who rode west, then south, and then east, coming back to the Rio Chama a few miles downstream from here where the river comes out of this canyon. When the sheriff followed the tracks to the river, he found a dead body leaning against a tree.

"The body wasn't more than two days old, so he figured it had to be one of the robbers. But the body had been mutilated. It had about twenty stab wounds, and it had been shot at least twelve times.

"Well, that didn't make any sense, so the sheriff wrapped the body in a blanket and took it to town. When the local doctor looked at it, the mystery deepened even more: The man's lungs were full of water; he had died from drowning. The knife and bullet wounds had occurred *after* he was dead."

"Uh-oh," said a guest.

"Wow," said another.

"The plot thickens," said a third.

"Okay, so the sheriff has a mysterious body on his hands, and he doesn't have a clue what happened. The next week, a trapper who had been catching beaver in the Rio Chama came into Tierra Amarilla with another body. Found on a sandbar a mile or so above the end of the canyon, this man had also drowned.

"But," Ted continued, "this body had a map on it."

"A map of what?" the guests asked.

"How'd the map survive the water?"

"Was it one of the bandits?"

"Well, I'll tell you," Ted continued, smiling sheepishly, clearly enjoying the storytelling. "The map was wrapped up in an oilskin sleeve, which kept it from getting wet. It was a hand-drawn map of the part of the canyon that we just happen to be sitting in right now. Ink lines showed each side of the canyon rim and a curvy line down the middle, which was more or less the path of the river.

"But," Ted grinned, "there was an X marked on the map. That X pointed to a location on the east side of the river, just about half a mile downstream from here."

"Ah, the famous X that marks the spot!" someone cried out.

"So now the sheriff has two bodies. He returns to the river canyon a couple of weeks after the robbery. The river was past flood stage by then, so he had no trouble using his horse to get up and down the canyon. Investigating where the X was located, and where the body was found, the sheriff also found the broken remains of a boat not a hundred yards further down. Now, it was common for ranchers to use small boats to cross the river, so he didn't connect it to the robbery until a couple days later when a railroad employee recognized the two dead men.

"The first body, the one that had been stabbed and shot, was Tom Coombs, a member of the track-laying gang of the railroad up in Chama. The second guy, the one with the map, was Everett Cossey. He had also worked laying track for the railroad.

"Tom Coombs was known to be a good worker, and Everett Cossey the same. But Everett had a brother named Orin, and Orin Cossey was well known to the railroad. He was a complainer, a bully, a lazy, no-account worker that nobody wanted anything to do with.

"Talking to some of the people that Coombs and Cossey had worked with, the sheriff decided that the two Cossey brothers, with Tom and two other workers from the train crew, had been the ones who had robbed the gold wagon. One robber was killed during the robbery—the sheriff had found his body when he found the wagon. He assumed that the others must have escaped down the valley on their horses.

"When the four outlaws got to where the Rio Cebolla joined the Chama, the gold was moved into the boat that the sheriff had found, and Everett Cossey took the boat down the river. The others rode off. The sheriff admitted that the move was clever and that he had been fooled; he had not imagined anyone splitting from the group and going down the river.

"Once in the canyon, Cossey buried the gold, marked the map, and then floated out of the canyon to meet the two other men, who had brought a third horse for him, which accounted for the three horse tracks that the sheriff had followed. He figured the men intended to ride off and then come back later to divide up the gold.

"At least that's what the sheriff thought was planned before things went wrong. The sheriff figured that after the gold was buried and Everett was back on the river, the boat overturned and he drowned. Since the river was at flood stage, that would have been highly likely.

"Of course, word got out, and hundreds of people rushed into the canyon to try to find the gold. The sheriff gave up trying to keep them out and even pasted the map in his office window because so many people were asking to see it. The place of the X, of course, was searched first, but nothing was found, so people started digging all up and down the canyon. The mania lasted for a month or so, and not a single coin was ever found. People went back to the river in the fall, when the water was at its lowest, searching for the gold in the riverbed itself. Nothing was found, and apparently none of the outlaws ever came back.

"Now, what about Tom Coombs' body being so mutilated after he had already drowned? Well, that's still a head scratcher. Since the body was found on the riverbank, propped up against a tree, it was assumed that Coombs had been one of the three riders that the sheriff had tracked to the river and that he had been killed by the other rider, who was probably Orin. The third horse would have been intended for Everett Cossey. But since Everett never came, Orin must have figured that his younger brother had died, so he left with all the horses.

"The stabbing and shooting of Tom never made any sense at all, so that's where the sheriff left it, as well as everybody else who investigated the robbery. There just wasn't a good explanation.

"So, that's where my tale ends—lost gold, mysterious deaths, a robbery gone bad, a body abused for no reason, and a mysterious map that points to nothing. A true New Mexico mystery, and you could be sitting right on top of the lost gold."

"What about the ghost?" a man asked.

"Ah, the ghost. Well, it wasn't too long before this canyon was considered haunted. A few people who were looking for the gold reported hearing cries in the night. Others reported screams and moans, plus the sound of thunderous water rushing by when the water was, in fact, calm. People have also reported seeing a man in the trees. He never says anything, never waves, and seems to vanish when people look closer. Odds are that it's the ghost of Everett Cossey, condemned to wander the river canyon forever."

A man in the trees, Mogi thought. "Do people say anything about him wandering around without a shirt?" he asked.

Ted looked up as the others turned to Mogi with questioning eyes.

"Well, I saw somebody today, some guy standing in the forest without a shirt on," Mogi said with a shrug. "His skin was really white, like he never got any sun."

CHAPTER

4

Mogi woke to birdsong. He could tell by the silvery light that the sun had not yet risen. He heard the soft, rhythmic sound of the river, which had been like a lullaby all night. While Jennifer slept soundly in her sleeping bag, he carefully unzipped the door of the tent.

No one was awake yet. Mogi stepped soundlessly away from the campsite and made his way down to the river. The sky was cloudless. He zipped up his jacket as a cool breeze greeted him at the water's edge. He found a soft hummock of grass and sat down.

A little splash in the center of the river told him there were fish there, probably trout. Ted had said the river was popular with fisherman and birders. The canyon was also home to cougars, black bears, badgers, coyotes, bobcats, mule deer, and even elk. It was such a special place, so close to towns and highways, yet so wild. He drank in the beauty for several minutes.

Then he saw movement from the corner of his eye. Movement, light and swift. He looked up and saw a bird in the distance, swooping toward the surface of the water.

It quickly flew back up and then alighted on a dead branch that stretched over the river. The bird repeated the motion several times as Mogi watched, transfixed.

Then the bird swept down fast, its long beak pointed toward the river not far from where Mogi was sitting. It dove just a few inches below the surface and came up with a fish in its beak. The silver fish glinted in the growing light, wriggling as the bird soared upriver. Mogi gasped.

Just then he heard voices from the campsite and a clatter of cooking pans. The sun peeked over the canyon wall. The moment had passed, but Mogi felt lucky beyond description to have experienced it.

What a place! he thought. It just oozes magic and spirit and beauty and I get to be right in the middle of it!

He stretched his arms and legs, thinking about how special the river and the canyon and the water and the trees were and that none of it should ever change.

A place like this, he was convinced, should last forever. As he rose, took a deep breath, and walked back to camp, he felt as if he were becoming part of the river.

The soft colors of the cool dawn were soon lost to the harsher light of the bright sun. After breakfast, eager to see more of the canyon, the group quickly broke camp and loaded the equipment onto the rafts.

The narrow walls of the canyon allowed the rafts to weave in and out of cool shadows, but it wasn't long before the sun moved overhead and there was no shade on the river. People were soon dipping their hats into the water and splashing themselves to fend off the heat.

An hour later, the river slowed as it left the narrow part of the canyon and began lazily winding back and forth across a broader valley floor. Wide meadows of tall grass led from the riverbank up to a line of sandy foothills that rambled along the foot of the cliffs.

As Mogi and Jennifer rowed the rafts through the calmer waters, buildings appeared on their left and Ted motioned for them to pull over.

At the base of the cliffs, they saw a number of low, mud-colored buildings alongside a single tall structure that stood out against the sandstone backdrop. The lower story of the structure had a single set of massive double doors and no windows whereas the walls of the second story were mostly glass. A narrow bell tower rose above it all even higher, topped by a thin cross.

"We're taking a little side trip," Ted said in a hushed tone as he gathered the group around the front of his raft. "This is the Monastery of Christ in the Desert, founded in 1964 and home to a group of Benedictine monks. We'll take a tour, but we have to be quiet."

Stepping around Sheila Winters as she filled yet another bottle of water, Mogi wrapped his bowline around the trunk of a cottonwood, took off his life jacket, and joined Jennifer as the group walked up a dirt road to a plaza in front of the tall building. A small bell hung in the center of the plaza. Ted rang it once to summon the guestmaster, a monk whose duties included greeting visitors.

As if he had already noticed the rafts and expected the group, a man dressed in a full-length robe, a hood pulled over his head, walked down a covered porch and joined them. Lowering his hood, the guestmaster smiled at the group and introduced himself in quiet tones as Brother Mark. He already knew Ted, and they shook hands amiably.

The rafters had arrived after lunch, which was served after Sunday mass and before midafternoon when the monks came together to sing and pray. This left the chapel, as they referred to the tall building, unoccupied, so Brother Mark led them through the door.

The effect was startling. After the intense sun and heat outside, the chapel's interior was quiet, solemn, and amazingly cool. The floor plan was in the shape of a square cross, the thick walls supporting the second story that held the windows on each side. The walls were hand-finished adobe, and the floor was made from flat stones that had been sealed and polished to a soft, rich luster. Hand-built chairs with high backs sat against two of the walls while low-back chairs were placed side by side across the floor. Several low benches framed the entryway. A wooden table in the center of the room held a tall silver cross.

Brother Mark formally greeted the visitors and told the story of a handful of monks who established the monastery a half century ago with only tents, mud huts, and outhouses. It now was home to a community of forty or more members of the Benedictine Order, housed in several buildings, plus a small convent for nuns. The abbot served as its leader.

The daily life of the monks began at four o'clock in the morning with Vigils, followed by regularly scheduled gatherings throughout the day for singing, praying, teaching, reading, and eating. Their day ended with a last gathering at 7:30, following by nightly silence. The in-between times were devoted to work, study, individual prayer, and recreation.

Brother Mark guided the visitors on a short tour of the facilities that were open to the public and ended with a visit to the gift shop, where products made by the monks were sold. As isolated as the monastery was—it was thirteen miles to the nearest highway on a road that was largely impassable in wet weather—the facilities included a large solar array for electricity, telephone service that included two hours of internet access every evening, a wastewater purification lagoon, and solar heating in most of the large rooms.

As the others wandered the gift shop, Mogi spoke quietly with Brother Mark.

"I saw a man in the woods yesterday," he said. "It seemed strange because we hadn't seen any other rafts. Do people hike into the canyon from somewhere around here?"

Brother Mark pursed his lips and looked thoughtful. "There are a few hikers who visit us, but they aren't allowed to enter the canyon area that's owned by the monastery. The Continental Divide Trail crosses the river a few miles below here, but it goes up onto the mesas and not down the canyon; that's typically the route the hikers take.

"You might have seen Brother Sebastian, however. He lives separately from the rest of us. He occupies a small cabin about a mile upriver. He has probably walked every square foot of the canyon valley and meditates in various places along the river. It might also have been another of our community. We're a pretty active group, and there are many trails used daily by our brothers."

That seemed reasonable to Mogi. He thanked the guestmaster and returned to the rafts. It was a lot easier to think he'd seen a monk than a ghost.

CHAPTER

5

"**C**an I help?" the woman at the front desk asked. It was Monday morning, and Jennifer was at the local library in Chama.

"Yes, ma'am," Jennifer replied. "I was wondering if you have any books with information about local robberies in the 1880s."

"Ah, I bet you want to know about the gold wagon robbery of 1882."

"How'd you know that?" Jennifer asked with a smile.

"Oh, everybody wants to know about that one. It's the most popular legend of Rio Arriba County. Let me show you what we have."

The librarian invited Jennifer behind the desk to a row of filing cabinets along the wall. The library was old, small, and largely devoted to children's books in both English and Spanish, though it provided a few shelves of hardcover and paperback books for adults.

"We get a lot of requests for information on the Cossey robbery. Every time some river guide tells the legend, there are one or two people who want the details. And, of course, everybody wants to see the map."

The librarian opened a filing cabinet and withdrew a large folder. Setting it on the corner of the desk, she opened the folder, removed a bundle of papers, and handed them to Jennifer.

"We have copies of original newspaper accounts and a few magazine articles, but this report is by far the best. We also have the original map, but we don't handle it much because it's pretty fragile. This report has a photocopy of it though, plus everything else that is known about the robbery."

Jennifer looked at the title on the first page. It was a college essay from somebody's history class.

"Lisa Quintana lives on a ranch outside of town," the librarian explained. "She went to the college down the road in El Rito, working on a history degree. For her senior research paper, she chose the Cossey robbery. After she graduated, we asked her if we could use her paper as a handout. We think she did an outstanding job."

Jennifer thumbed through it. There was a lot more about the robbery than Ted had told, plus photographs and a couple of drawings. As she thumbed through the pages, the map quickly drew her eye. A full-page reproduction, the photocopy not only had the clearly defined lines of the canyon rims and river, but reflected the folds, wrinkles, creases, tears, smudges, and dirt that must have been part of the original. It looked old in spite of its being a copy.

"They drew the map on the back of an old wanted poster," the librarian explained, pulling a plastic sleeve from the folder. "This is the original."

Jennifer's eyes widened in surprise as she carefully took the plastic sleeve from the woman and looked at the faded brown paper it contained. The actual map found on the dead body in 1882!

The original was half the size of the reproduction. It was brown, much like a paper grocery sack, with splotches and stains. The crumpled and worn paper was creased in several places where it had been folded. The edges were ragged, and the corners had several small tears.

The drawing of the river was easy to make out, and the surrounding contours of the cliffs were distinct. There was also an X, just as Ted had described.

"Nobody's ever found any gold or anything?"

"Not a penny," the librarian said with a smile. "There's usually at least one person every summer who thinks they've figured out the mystery and they go hunting for it, but so far nobody's gotten rich."

"Anybody ever go in with excavators or backhoes? I mean, some people would be crazy enough if they thought they could find a hundred pounds of gold."

The woman laughed. "The river corridor, from the base of the canyon on one side to the base on the other side, is a wilderness area, so you couldn't take big machinery in even if you were that crazy. You're not even supposed to take in metal detectors. The monastery owns the last mile and a half of the canyon, so you couldn't get anything noisy past them anyway. Of course, not all of the river is so protected."

"What happened to all of the historical land owners along the river? I remember seeing the one old house, but I thought people would have divided up this river-front land a long time ago."

"Oh, most of the land around this part of New Mexico was given to settlers in big blocks by either Spanish or Mexican land grants. Through the years, various parts were sold as individual ranches, but there just haven't been many people in this part of the state. It wasn't until the '40s that we even got paved roads around here. We're a little remote."

"Well, my mom sure loves it up here. Give her an opportunity to buy land and she'd fall all over herself for a piece."

"If she hurries," the librarian said, "she might get one of the last big pieces. There's been a big tract, 1,100 acres, on the market for a couple of years that's just about to be sold. Have you been on the river? You know where the monastery is?"

Jennifer nodded.

"The tract is on the west side of the Chama, catty-corner from the monastery. It's probably the most prime piece of property to come up for sale in a long time since it's so close to Georgia O'Keeffe's house and to Ghost Ranch. But your Mom had better hurry—I hear some lady from California is set to buy it.

"In fact," she added, glancing out the window, "there she is now."

Jennifer followed the librarian's gaze out the library window. A woman and two men were standing in front of a realty office across the street, talking. A few moments later, the two men climbed into a black Suburban and the woman got into a smaller car.

Jennifer took a sharp breath. It was Sheila Winters.

*   *   *

"I guess she can buy land if she wants to," Mogi said.

"On a teacher's salary?" Jennifer shot back. "The librarian showed me the listing—it's $6.4 million! I didn't think it made any sense, so wait till you hear what I did. After I got the report from the librarian, I Googled Sheila Winters' name. It turns out she's not a biology teacher."

"She's not?"

"Nope. Sheila Winters is the president and CEO of LottaWatta of California."

It was Monday afternoon. Mogi had spent the morning helping Ted clean the rafts, life jackets, and other equipment and stowing it all away in the maintenance shed. The work was his trade-off with Jennifer if she would go into Chama to get more information on the Cossey robbery. He couldn't help but be interested in a story of lost treasure.

"What's LottaWatta?" he asked.

"I'm glad you asked. LottaWatta of California is a company that bottles and sells water. It's located in the San Joaquin Valley, north of Bakersfield."

"Okay. So what?"

"This is what. I did a little snooping in the newspapers in Bakersfield. You know that California, like most of the Southwest, is in a terrible drought. It's lasted for several years now, and the reservoirs that feed the big cities are at like 5 percent of what's needed to keep up with demand.

"The whole San Joaquin Valley, which is agricultural, doesn't have close to the amount of water needed for irrigating crops. The rivers that feed the valley, plus all the water they pump from below ground, isn't enough, and the water they get from the Colorado River is way below normal, too, because the snowpack and rains on the Colorado Plateau have been so much less than usual."

"No kidding," Mogi said. "Even the San Juan River has been lower than usual. What's this got to do with Sheila Winters?"

"Duh! She owns LottaWatta, a bottling plant that sells bottled water all over the United States, and which just happens to get its water from California reservoirs. When some newspaper did an exposé on the operation, there was a big push to shut her down. Californians don't take kindly to a corporation profiting from selling California's precious water to people in New York or Florida.

"The bottom line is that she's been forced out of business because they won't let her have the water anymore. She stands to lose a load of money if she can't relocate."

Mogi was silent, and then his eyes grew big. He looked at Jennifer.

"Wait, are you thinking she's buying that land on the Chama so she can move a bottling plant here? Where would she. . .wait a minute! Are you thinking she wants to take water out of the Rio Chama?"

"That's my guess," Jennifer said. "She's not taking water samples back to some biology class. I think she's taking the water back to have it analyzed so she can filter it, bottle it, and sell it."

Mogi sat back in the porch swing of their casita, stunned, remembering that beautiful morning, the cool quiet, the bird and his fish—what would happen to the canyon?

Jennifer finally ended her pacing and sat down beside him.

"She can't do that," he said. "There are laws against it, aren't there?"

"The librarian said that while a lot of the river and the canyon are protected, not all of it is. If she owns the land, I bet she gets the water rights to go with it. If she needs more, all she has to do is make a plea to the state government that she's moving a multi-million-dollar business to New Mexico, which we know is always desperate for jobs. I bet she'd get whatever she wants. At least she probably thinks she can."

They sat in silence for a while.

"Besides ruining the awesomeness of the river and the canyon, do you realize what this would do to the monastery?" Mogi asked. "They live in a pristine canyon because of the peace and quiet. They're miles and miles from anywhere because the solitude and silence are key to their way of life. If there were a bottling plant on the other side of the river. . .well, remember that big bridge we floated under? It's the only way to get across the river. Big trucks going back and forth all day long would destroy the quiet of the canyon."

"The monastery and its way of life would cease to exist," Jennifer added.

And everything I felt that morning, sitting on the river bank, Mogi thought, would also cease to exist.

CHAPTER

"**O**h, I don't think I'd worry about it," Ted said as he saddled a horse for a Monday evening horseback ride. "Why pick New Mexico for water? We're suffering as much as California, though maybe not on their scale. If I were going to build a water-bottling plant, I'd pick Tennessee or someplace that has a lot of water."

Mogi and Jennifer were disappointed by Ted's reaction. In their minds, Sheila Winters was a genuine threat. She had obviously kept her real identity and purpose hidden, she had gathered water samples from the river, and she had big money and a powerful corporation behind her. Whatever she was planning, it involved the Rio Chama's water and the land that she was buying. Six-plus million dollars was serious money, and if she weren't after the water, what else could she be doing?

Mogi hated unanswered questions, but it didn't look like he was going to get any satisfaction. Reminding themselves that they were only visitors, the brother and sister went back to work.

The Franklin family was well regarded at Ghost Ranch. Mrs. Franklin was a big hit with the seminar attendees, and Mogi and Jennifer had been recognized as good workers who were a pleasure to have around—they smiled a lot and worked hard, just like their mom.

At the beginning of the second week, they were given more options—they could either work with the horses or in the kitchen. Jennifer, who was not a fan of working out in the sun if she could avoid it, began helping the kitchen staff prepare food and drinks and also washed dishes. A lot of dishes.

Mogi began helping Ted and the wranglers care for the horses and get them ready for the various rides offered at the ranch. He also took care of the tack—saddles, bridles, halters, and blankets. He worked in the garden when he didn't have other work to do.

The threat of the water bottling plant drifted to the back of their minds. Getting up every morning and absorbing the beauty of the wide valley couldn't help but reinforce Ted's observation—this high, dry, semi-desert mountainous country was not the place anyone would go looking for large amounts of water to export.

One evening, while Mrs. Franklin was busy preparing her presentation for the next day, Mogi lay on his bed looking at Lisa Quintana's research paper as Jennifer got back from working in the kitchen.

"Find anything interesting?" Jennifer asked.

"I'd like to go and see the original map."

"There are a lot of details in the paper that Ted didn't mention, but I'm not sure any of them change the story. The bank in Denver hired the Pinkerton Detective Agency to investigate the robbery. They didn't reach any conclusions either but wrote a detailed report about what they discovered. Lisa Quintana included it as an appendix to her paper."

Jennifer continued, "Did you know they found a rope that was later confirmed to have been tied to the boat that was found? They found it coiled up on a bank, as if it had been deliberately taken off the boat and used for something. That's a little fishy. What would Everett Cossey have done with a rope? Why leave it on the bank instead of tying it back on? And when they looked at the boat itself, do you know what they found?"

"I give up."

"The boat's bottom had been bashed in, like it had struck a rock or something. Cossey tried to fix it by stuffing his shirt into the crack and pounding the boards back into place. That would have required pulling the boat out of the river to turn it over and work on it. Now, he might have already buried the gold before he did this, but it's more likely that the boat was bashed first and then dragged out of the water. That would have required taking all the gold out of the boat, so if that were the case, he probably buried everything somewhere close rather than putting it back into the damaged boat. He would have just marked the map at a different place."

"Wait," Mogi interrupted. "What about his shirt?"

"The shirt? He stuffed it into the crack, and—"

"So when he died, he didn't have a shirt on."

"Right. If he put the boat back into the river after fixing it, he wouldn't have had a shirt on when he died."

Mogi felt a chill run up his spine.

*　　*　　*

The summer rains had begun. Mornings were bright and sunny and the air hot before ten o'clock. Small clouds appeared over the mountains by noon, and by early afternoon, a thick line of thunderheads stretched across the valley with dark sheets of rain falling beneath.

After he finished his morning work with the horses, Mogi walked to the maintenance shed and looked across the wide expanse of mountains opposite the Ghost Ranch property. The tops of the thunderheads rolled and spread as they advanced, and curtains of water slowly moved across the plains. Within an hour, small drops spotted the sidewalks, then larger drops, and finally a thick, hard-hitting, slapping rain gushed from the sky.

Mogi timed it so that he was safe under the porch of the dining hall before the hard rain began. The smell of the rain hit as hard as the drops, and he laughed at how surprising the storm seemed in spite of his having watched it form. It was a "male" rain, he thought—sudden, powerful, almost angry in its pounding of the ground. That was what the Navajo called it. A "female" rain was softer, quieter, more of a steady drizzle. Either way, the rain was a blessing, and he knew it should always be appreciated.

Less than an hour later, the rain slowed, sputtered, and then became a mist that dried up as the clouds lightened, separated, and disappeared, letting the sun again dominate the sky. Only the puddles on the sidewalks and the new mud in the roads gave a hint of what had just happened.

The monsoon weather system forced the horseback rides and van tours at the ranch to operate only during the morning hours or after supper. This schedule kept Mogi busy from before breakfast to about noon, first putting all the necessary equipment on the horses, and then taking it all off. The early evening was a repeat of the morning routine, leaving his afternoons mostly free. He followed Ted around and helped with whatever he could. Jennifer had no lack of work, regardless of the rain. The kitchen was always busy preparing meals, serving meals, cleaning up after meals, and then starting the routine all over again. It was hard work, and Jennifer was amazed at how relaxed the cooks were in spite of the large number of guests that had to be fed. During the week, depending on which groups were at the ranch, up to a hundred and fifty hungry mouths came through the door three times a day. On the weekends, the numbers could swell to more than two hundred.

"You're reading the Pinkerton report," Mogi said as he came into the casita after caring for the horses from the evening ride.

"Yep," Jennifer said. "Nothing else to do. I'm too tired to go to bed, and it's fun reading. I'm impressed with those guys. They must have been the CSI of their day and were also into criminal profiling. What they wrote about the Cossey brothers is pretty in depth and just fascinating. They must have interviewed a hundred people to get the information.

"Orin was a classic bully. He never cut Everett any slack, was always insulting him, embarrassing him, treating him like dirt while Everett played the role of the hurt puppy. When the Pinkertons traced their past history in Texas and Colorado, it was always Orin who laid the plans, Orin who played the lead role, Orin who cheated the people while Everett stood around looking guilty when they were caught.

"Which didn't win them friends, by the way. The Pinkertons never talked to anyone who was friendly toward the Cosseys, not even toward Everett by himself. Orin looked down on everybody, didn't want friends, and seemed to not even want Everett."

Jennifer got to her feet and strode from one side of the room to the other.

"Everett looked stupid compared to his brother. Orin could read; Everett couldn't. Orin could write; Everett couldn't. Orin was tall and good-looking; Everett was short and unattractive. Everett talked about his momma back home in Arkansas, Orin never. And Orin could be physically rough on his brother—witnesses saw Orin beat Everett when he made even a minor mistake, beat him like a dog. But Everett never left his brother and followed him wherever he wanted to go, no matter what."

Mogi listened closely to what she said. If there were anything that could get Jennifer stirred up, it was abuse. When she saw it, she called it out.

Orin Cossey was a big bully.

"And I'll tell you something else," Jennifer continued, taking a seat on the bed, clutching the paper in her hands. "Orin Cossey would never have divided up the gold among the whole gang. Even if it were the people he had recruited to rob the pay wagon, he would *never* have considered that the gold belonged to anybody but him."

CHAPTER

7

It looks like you may have been more right than what I gave you credit for."

Ted was already at the horse barn when Mogi arrived on Wednesday morning.

"What do you mean?" Mogi asked through a yawn, bringing over a horse to be rubbed down before the saddle blanket and saddle were strapped on.

"I went to Bode's General Store in Abiquiu late yesterday to get supplies," Ted said. "Several of the ranchers were talking about their new neighbor. Seems the deal for the land on the Chama was filed at the county courthouse on Monday and, first thing yesterday morning, a couple of trucks and a tractor showed up at that bridge on the river. Well, somebody cut the lock and they went across, headed up toward the Rio Gallina, which is across from the lower boundary of the monastery. What's interesting is that one truck was a big drilling rig."

"Drilling rig? What for?"

"Maybe to find out what the rock structure looks like under the topsoil, which in itself is not unusual—any owner of a piece of ranch property wants to know if they're sitting on sand or clay or bedrock or sandstone, just for the sake of confirming their mineral rights. But the geology of this valley is pretty well known from the building of the Abiquiu Dam years ago. It required all sorts of sampling to be done across the valley floor.

"Rushing to drill seems like they're awfully anxious to know about something in particular, not to mention that everybody is expecting the land to be left in pasture. What's under the surface shouldn't be that concerning to the new owner unless maybe they want to know the water level."

"What are the ranchers saying?"

"Oh, mainly that they're going to complain that nobody represented them in the negotiations. The land's been used for grazing cattle for the last century or so, and some of the ranchers probably had long-time grazing agreements with previous owners. Now it looks like they're going to lose access to all that grass. That could be significant for those with a lot of cattle. The grass around here is pretty thin—it takes a lot of land to provide enough grass for a herd."

"So, everything seems like it's going to happen?"

"There's a ten-day waiting period before the sale is completed. That gives the current owner time to make sure that the finances are true and gives the future owner time to examine the land, do tests, look at the grass, check the history, or any other kind of exploration. If something is out of sorts, or even if anybody just gets nervous, the ten days gives either the buyer or the seller a chance to back out. If nothing like that happens, it's a done deal a week from today."

When the horses were saddled and tied up along the corral fence, Ted and Mogi walked to the dining hall for breakfast and then returned to greet the guests as they arrived for the morning ride. Mogi recognized most of them—it was the same group that had gone rafting, taking another break from the seminar. They recognized him and several slapped him on the back for being brave enough to go adventuring with them again.

Sheila Winters greeted him with a smile, and Ted brought her a horse that was gentle and not too tall.

It would be a two-hour ride. Ted would lead them at a leisurely pace for a couple of miles until they came to the box canyon where a stream poured from a split in the canyon wall. Following a trail of switchbacks out of the canyon and onto the plateau above the Ghost Ranch facilities, they would ride along the edges of the mesas to take photographs and then loop back, going down the switchbacks and arriving back at the corral in time for lunch.

Mogi followed the group, riding the last horse. He was an experienced rider but had not been up the trail nor taken any of the official rides. The group, as with the rafting trip, had requested a custom trip, and the wranglers were accommodating the request though it left them shorthanded; that's why Ted had recruited him.

He was more than happy to help out.

*　*　*

Sheila Winters was not a horse person.

Ted had always impressed Mogi with his easy-going ways, but his knowledge of horses truly set him apart from the other wranglers. Though there were more than a hundred horses at Ghost Ranch, enough for the guests as well as the cowboys who managed the sixteen-thousand acre ranch on horseback, Ted seemed to know all of them— their coloring, their temperaments, their ages, and their handling when bridled and saddled. This gave him good insight when it came to matching particular horses to particular guests.

With only a look at a person and a couple of questions, Ted would choose a horse that fit the person's ability and comfort level. Mogi thought he had found a good one for Sheila.

But Sheila would have disagreed. She found her horse to be slow, and not quick enough to obey her commands. Within a few minutes, it was obvious she believed the horse needed to know that she was in charge.

She gathered the leather reins close to the horse's neck so that his head was pulled down and then used the remaining portion of the reins as a whip, hitting the horse on the rump when she wanted to catch up to the others, but also against the horse's shoulder in punishment for being what she considered slow to obey. She would kick her heels into the horse's side to speed him up, and then pull violently against the reins to slow him down. The horse's head would then kick up, causing him to snort and struggle.

It was painful for Mogi to watch. If she would just relax and let the horse do what he was trained to do, everything would be fine.

But she would not. Ted was far in the lead and, with the twisting trail, could not see what was happening. Mogi decided that he could help. He pulled up closer to her and said, "Ma'am, if you'll loosen the reins, he'd—"

"Don't tell me what to do, boy!" Sheila snarled at him. "I can handle a stupid horse."

Mogi backed off.

The group made it to the end of the box canyon. They let their horses drink the cold water and then started up the switchbacks. Mogi wanted to say something again to Sheila but decided against it. He was only a volunteer. Who was he to speak up?

It was at the top of the switchbacks that Ted got involved.

Switchbacks, zigzagging trails that move back and forth across the slope of a hill, allow a horse and rider to go steadily up the incline without the trail becoming too steep. Switchbacks in rocky canyon country are typically well worn but narrow, with edges that can crumble. Horses know this, and Mogi was sure that every horse at Ghost Ranch had been over these trails enough that they knew exactly where to place their hooves to make the climb as safe and unexciting as possible.

But Sheila Winters thought she knew better.

Continuing with the shortening of the reins, refusing to allow the horse's head to stretch out, she stood up in her stirrups and leaned forward. Using her hand to push against the horse's head, she pushed back and forth as she rocked above the saddle. She held her body as if she were on the pedals of a bike going uphill, digging in for more bite against the road. She yelled into the horse's ears, cursed him, and repeatedly slapped the reins against his shoulder.

Mogi watched the horse get frustrated and angry, speeding up at times to nudge against the horse in front of it. The trail being narrow, the horse ahead would stutter in its steps, pushing back against being hurried. Her horse would then snap its head up and try to push by on the other side.

Mogi was scared that one of the horses would step on an edge of the trail and it would crumble beneath its hoof, or that the rear horse would push the horse in front over the edge. He also feared that either horse would rear up, lose its footing, and tumble backward, making the rider slide off and tumble down the side of the trail onto the steep slope.

Those things did not happen, but at the top of the trail where the last switchback came out onto the flat mesa top, Sheila's horse had had enough. It shook its head violently and bucked, sending her flying into the dirt and sagebrush.

Ted rushed to her and helped her to her feet, but suffered a verbal attack that would have knocked an ordinary man down. She was as mad as anyone Mogi had ever seen.

She let Ted know exactly what she thought of that dumb horse, that dumb trail, and the stupidity of Ghost Ranch for putting its guests in danger. Before he could stop her, she grabbed a fist-sized rock and threw it at the horse.

Ted stopped talking and grabbed her hand before she could throw another rock.

Mogi dismounted and rushed to help. He knew it hurt to be bucked off, and he honestly hoped she wasn't injured, even though she had caused it. But when she went after Ted and Ghost Ranch, Mogi wished for the horse to come back and kick her in the behind. When she threw the rock, he felt ready to do it himself.

Ted was diplomatic. He had been watching as the horse train came up the switchbacks, and he could see that Sheila was handling the horse wrong. He had intended to move her closer to the front of the train and give her some suggestions.

It was now too late for suggestions. Without saying a word to her, he led her to Mogi's horse, had him mount up, and then helped Sheila up behind him.

"Take her back to the corral. Go slow on the way down," was all he said, and walked away.

It felt like a long time getting back. Sheila continued her ranting and cursing, and he was grateful to finally get to the corral and help her down from behind the saddle.

"You come with me, boy," she said. Mogi obeyed.

She marched up the sidewalk to her casita and he waited patiently as she threw her things into two suitcases. Handing the luggage to him in a huff, she pointed to a parking lot in the distance and told him she would join him there after she went to the office to get a refund for the days she was not going to spend in her room.

"I'm done with this place. They only want people who are used to putting up with bad service."

That's not the reason, Mogi thought, but was silent as he rolled the suitcases down the sidewalk.

Fifteen minutes later, Sheila Winters was driving away. Mogi watched, thinking about what had happened over the past hour and how he wanted to tell Jennifer every detail. He especially wanted to tell her about the woman's eyes.

After she was thrown off, Sheila Winters' face distorted with rage. Mogi had been shocked at the intensity—her skin suddenly a deep red, her chin jutting forward, her teeth bared, her eyes narrowed. When she threw the rock, her eyes glowed with a deep-seated anger and revenge that he had never before seen in a human face.

It was a rage that could have murdered.

CHAPTER

8

It was Thursday morning. No horse trips were scheduled, so Mogi returned to the ever-present work in the garden. He was surprised when Ted showed up.

"You too busy for a break?" he asked.

"I'm never too busy for a break. Whatcha got?"

"Let's go for a ride. I want to check out something that might interest you."

That sounded mysterious enough, but after they left Ghost Ranch in one of the ranch pickups and immediately turned onto the dirt road to the monastery, Mogi was even more puzzled.

The rains had made the road muddy enough in a few places that the pickup slid back and forth a few times. Ted focused on keeping it steady. Thirty minutes later, he pulled over at the single bridge that went over the Rio Chama.

"We'll walk from here," Ted said as he ducked under the pipe gate that blocked the roadway. Someone must have replaced the lock that was broken by the drill rig on Tuesday.

"This is the land that Sheila Winters is buying, right?" Mogi asked as they stepped off the bridge onto a more primitive dirt road.

"Yup. The property runs over to the mesas on the west, and then up to the Rio Gallina. It makes pretty much a square across from the monastery's southern boundary."

They walked about a half-mile along the dirt road before they veered to the left, following deep tread marks. A couple of hundred yards farther, Ted motioned for Mogi to come closer and pointed to a pipe sticking out of the dirt.

The soil around the pipe had been scraped back, forming a shallow depression about thirty yards in diameter. It was mostly a dry mud flat streaked with large tire tracks crisscrossing the width, with a small pool of water still visible in the center. A spotty band of white, chalky soil circled the depression, indicating that the pool had been much larger.

"That white stuff around the circle is a mineral ring," Ted said. "The water that formed this pool had to have had a high mineral content to leave a ring like that. I expect that the rig drilled into a layer of calcite or gypsum or something and then struck water that squirted up the pipe."

Ted walked around the flat area, avoiding the mud until he was close to the pipe. "Whoever was drilling wanted to get deep enough to confirm what they were looking for. They drilled until they hit water, let it run enough to flood this depression, and then closed it off."

"So, they *are* after the water, aren't they?"

"Not exactly. They're not after the water so they can bottle it. They want it because it's hot."

"Huh?"

Ted looked at him. "Remember the hot springs across from the old Martinez place? That area has water that has squeezed through a series of cracks in the hot rocks below, heated up, and then found a path to the surface. On this property, since there're no natural hot springs, a drilling rig was brought in to see how far down they'd have to drill to find that layer of really hot rock. It doesn't look like it was very far."

"Sheila Winters wants to build a spa?" Mogi guessed.

Ted laughed. "Not likely. Over in Abiquiu, one of the ranchers had looked up the company whose name was written on the side of the drill rig. It's a geothermal research company, which means that somebody's thinking about building a hot-water electrical generation plant."

Mogi was instantly reminded of something he'd seen near Jemez Springs, a little town about sixty miles south and west from Ghost Ranch. At a summer camp in the Jemez Mountains, he and Jennifer had gone on a tour of a geothermal facility that pumped liquid into the ground, let it heat up, pumped it back up, let the hot liquid boil water into steam, and then used the steam to drive turbines, producing electricity. It was a lot like a regular power plant.

"Wow," was all Mogi could say.

"It would be quite a deal," Ted continued. "There are power lines that connect to the dam at Abiquiu Lake not twenty miles from here. A new plant could plug right into the electrical grid without much work at all. It's a fairly green technology, so it would be viewed favorably by the legislature, and it would create jobs, which is always popular.

"And it would destroy this entire valley," he said.

Ted turned and Mogi had to hurry to keep up with his long strides back to the pickup.

CHAPTER
9

Ted dropped Mogi at the Franklins' casita. It was close enough to lunch that he could have gone to the dining hall, but Mogi wasn't hungry, and when his appetite failed him, he knew something was wrong.

He sat at the writing table with his chin in his hands and tried to understand two separate stories that were making him feel stupid.

The first story was about Sheila Winters.

On the one hand, jobs were good, and using the earth's heat to produce electricity was good.

On the other hand, an electrical generation plant—an industrial plant of any kind—would destroy the beauty and the raw wildness of the Rio Chama, its canyon, and the valley below it. Would that be worth the trade-off? Why did the plant have to be in this valley? Why not drill near the Four Corners Generating Station, the coal-fired power plant up near Shiprock? It was famous for its pollution—why not put a hot rock generation plant up there and shut down the coal plant? The people living there were already used to having a power plant, and the new one would be quieter and cleaner. Couldn't Sheila Winters buy land up there?

The geology is too different, Mogi guessed. The rock structure beneath the surface wasn't hot enough, or it was too far down.

Sheila must have known about the hot springs along the river before she came to Ghost Ranch, so her purchasing the land had to have been in the works for a year or longer. Why was she choosing now to buy? Because of the worsening drought in California?

The second story was about the Cossey brothers.

It was a lot less serious, but it had been percolating in the back of his brain. He couldn't get all the pieces to fit in their puzzle, and it was irritating him. Overall, it was clever—and original—to hide the gold in the canyon. If Everett hadn't drowned getting out, the plan would have worked.

But why was that other man, already dead from drowning, also stabbed and shot? Does the rope left on the riverbank mean anything? Why had Everett marked the wrong place on the map?

Mogi found the photocopy of the map and laid it on the desk.

Amazing, he thought. It was a hundred and how many years old? The original must have been touched hundreds of times before the copy was made, yet the lines still looked pretty good. And the X looked. . . .

Wait a minute. The X looked straight, clear, and well written.

But Everett Cossey didn't know how to write. Not that he couldn't make an X, but a hand not used to printing wouldn't have made one so clear.

The X and the whole map, for that matter, were drawn in ink. In 1882, that meant dipping a pen into an ink bottle. But Everett Cossey didn't have a pen or an ink bottle—they would have been in his pockets when he was found, and the report said there was nothing in his pockets. He might have thrown them away, but still, could he have written the X so well, without blots, without quivering lines, with hands dirty from digging, after riding a boat through a flooding river and dragging it up on the bank?

Mogi looked at the whole map: the long lines used for the Chama, the Cebolla, and the Gallina; the short lines used to show contours; and the lines depicting the canyon rim. They were all even and straight—the same width and clearly drawn. Exactly like the X.

Mogi sat back, puzzling over what seemed to be a common sense conclusion: Everett had not drawn the X—it must have been put on the map at the same time the map was drawn. That meant that Orin (it had to be Orin) drew both the map and the X before Everett ever launched the boat, before the gold was ever put in the boat, before the robbery ever took place.

If Mogi was confused before, he was even more confused now.

Orin Cossey must *really* have not trusted his brother. The plan must have been for Everett to take the gold down the river, stop at the location of the X, bury the gold, meet at the end of the canyon, and then ride on. Orin didn't even trust him to mark the map to show the location.

Or, maybe Orin knew that if Everett had to mark the map, he would have needed a pen and an ink bottle to mark it, or a pencil, or something, and he didn't want him to carry them.

Or, maybe the map was needed to show to the other members of the gang. The X would show each of them where the gold was going to be buried.

Nah, Mogi thought, Orin would never have revealed that. He would have bullied everybody into supposedly trusting him, and—

Wait a minute.

Everett would not have had to bury the gold at the X in any case. In fact, Everett would not have had to bury the gold at all.

Mogi realized that Jennifer had been absolutely right—Orin Cossey would never have shared the gold in the first place. And if that were true, the whole business of the gang escaping with the gold had been staged.

The map was a fake.

CHAPTER

10

"**A** power plant? She wants to build a power plant?" Jennifer asked.

"Well, maybe, maybe not."

"Okay, right-brain boy, explain it to me. I thought you just said that she was drilling to find out how close to the surface the hot rock was so that a power plant could be built."

"Correct. But if she can just show it to be possible, then, according to what Ted is thinking, she'd probably do all the preliminaries herself, like preparing the locals for the idea, getting the politicians in line, and so forth, and then sell the land to a power company who would do the actual building. She'd make a lot of money, quick and easy."

"Hmm. . .okay. That makes more sense for someone like her. She seems more like a profiteer than a pioneer. So a power company would do the work?"

"Yeah," Mogi continued. "It would take new roads, electrical substations, huge water tanks, big-as-a-house turbines, massive electrical cables running across huge towers, and cooling ponds for the steam. There'd be cars and trucks going back and forth all day long, and the noise and smell would carry into every part of the countryside. The whole valley would be ruined."

"I don't like the sound of this. Regardless of getting green energy, destroying the river and the canyon isn't right. Does Ted think anything can be done about it?"

"Ted wasn't in the mood to talk about that part of it, so I don't know, but I guess somebody would have to take the power company to court to prevent them from building. That would take a lot of money up front, and you might have to fight the politicians who want investment and jobs coming into the state."

"Ghost Ranch could sue, I guess," Jennifer said, "but it's miles away. The monastery has the strongest argument against a plant, I would think, but it's not like a monastery would have the money it would take to wage a legal war. I don't know what they would do."

"Well, what if they, you know, uh, had that kind of money, like, well, a hundred and fifty pounds of, uh, gold. Then, uh, maybe. . . ."

Jennifer looked at Mogi, drew a chair from across the room, and sat directly in front of him. "Don't tell me that you've found the buried treasure. You haven't. I've been with you every day since you've been here, and I haven't seen you carrying around any bags of gold or even a shovel to dig them up with. I also know you haven't found any new clues that suddenly popped up after a hundred and fifty years because you couldn't possibly keep it to yourself."

Mogi grinned. "I have a new clue."

Jennifer hung her head, shaking it in disbelief. "Oh, Lord, give me strength," she said quietly. "Okay. Go ahead.

Tell me and get it over with. Let's not mention it to Mom yet, okay? The poor woman has already suffered enough from our adventures. Tell me about the clue."

"I'm so glad you asked!" Mogi said, grinning. He led her through his observations of the map and the idea that it was a fake.

"So, the map is a fake?"

"Yes. I think Orin Cossey never intended for the gold to be buried at all. He created the map for two reasons: First, he needed something to show to the other gang members so they would be convinced that for all the effort of sending the gold down the river, it would indeed result in it being buried. In that case, the X probably isn't where the gold was buried since any one of them could sneak back and dig it up. The X is probably where they were going to meet up later. I don't know if it even meant anything.

"Second, Orin needed the map so it could be placed on a dead body at the end of the canyon. In that case, he wanted the sheriff to think that it *had* been buried, and the X was the location."

"Orin was going to kill Everett?"

"No, no. The dead body with the map on it was going to be Tom Coombs. That's why Coombs came back to the river with Orin. He was probably told that they were going to get Everett, which is why Orin had to bring a third horse. But Orin drowns him instead, planning that when Everett comes out of the canyon, they would bash a hole in the boat, tuck the map in Coombs' belt, and stage things so the sheriff would think that Tom had buried the gold in the canyon and then drowned on the way out."

"And then Orin and Everett escape with the gold."

"That's right. Since Tom is dead, his horse could be used to carry the bags of gold. Orin probably planned on them going to Mexico and living like kings. And all the while, people would be in a frenzy looking for the gold in the canyon and would forget about chasing the bandits."

"Well, keeping the gold is certainly what Orin would have done, according to the Pinkerton description."

"Absolutely. Well," Mogi continued, "if Orin is expecting Everett to come straight through the canyon with a boat full of gold, think about what Everett does when he accidentally crashes the boat. He tries to repair the boat but panics because he believes the boat will no longer hold both him and the gold. He decides to take the gold out of the boat and bury it after all, hoping that his fix will be enough to get him to Orin, and that Orin will think that Everett did the right thing, given the accident.

"But he knows that Orin doesn't trust him, so he's got to give him some sort of directions to it. He has to make some kind of mark to show where it is. He's got the map, but he doesn't have a pen or pencil, so he has to do something to mark where he actually buried the gold. Maybe he scratches a sign on a tree trunk, or makes a stack of rocks, or maybe chips out an X on the side of a cliff— whatever. The mark has to be something that anybody might see but would be recognized only by him and Orin when they return to get the gold."

Jennifer leaned back in the chair and folded her arms above her head. "I think you've got that right. Everett has got to do something, to make a mark that Orin will understand. That all makes sense. Now what?"

"We have to go back to the canyon."

Jennifer laughed. "Wait a minute. This is where we started. There have been hundreds of people looking for that gold for more than a hundred and thirty years. Now you think that the map being a fake is going to help you find the gold?"

"We're not going to look for the gold," Mogi said, tilting his head to the side.

"We're not looking for the gold? So, why do we need to go back to the canyon?" Jennifer asked, her eyebrows raised.

"Well, all these years, everyone has been looking for the gold. We're not going to look for the gold. We're going to look for Everett's mark. He had to do something that would have lasted. I think people have walked right by it all this time and never knew what they were looking at."

CHAPTER

11

It was eight o'clock the next morning, Friday. As Jennifer and Mogi drove the Franklin family car out to the monastery, Ted followed in the ranch truck. They left the car in the monastery parking lot and then Ted gave them a ride up to the village of Cebolla, turning west onto a dirt road that ran along the Rio Cebolla and ended at a fenced pasture. Their plan was to walk down the Rio Cebolla, hit the Rio Chama, and then walk down the river to their car parked at the monastery.

When Ted dropped them off, watching him turn the ranch pickup around and disappear over the rise gave Mogi an unexpected feeling of being abandoned.

"I'm glad you didn't have to work," he said to Jennifer as they picked their way through the grass and weeds along the bank of the Rio Cebolla.

"Well, I'll have to make up the hours this weekend. Remind me why we had to do this today?"

"We need the water level of the Chama to be low so we can walk down the riverbed and wade across the river if we need to," Mogi said. "Ted said water from the dam is released only on weekends to save water for irrigation in the late summer. So, today being Friday, there's hardly any water in the river. Sometime this afternoon, the dam will let out more water so the river will fill up and people can go rafting like we did last weekend. On Sunday afternoon, they'll crank the water back down for the rest of the week.

"Besides, Mom wants us to go with her to Santa Fe tomorrow, and I just couldn't wait until next week. I have the feeling we're going to find something really significant."

When Mogi and Jennifer reached the Chama, they were where Everett Cossey had left Orin and the other gang members and took the boat down the river. Someplace after that, Everett had stashed the stolen gold.

Once they began following the Chama, there was no getting back to the car without walking the whole distance; they were on their own. Mogi judged the distance to be not much more than a longish hike. He figured it would be an all-day effort, but not very difficult.

He was wrong.

*   *   *

"It's hot. I didn't know it would be this hot," Mogi said.

It was almost noon. The brother and sister had been hiking for nearly three hours.

"I thought you'd have a better idea of what kind of mark we'd be looking for," Jennifer answered back, not disguising her growing disgust at being talked into this wild goose chase. "You had no idea, did you?"

Mogi huffed. "Well, I was sure he didn't have a bucket of paint to put great big arrows on the rocks that said, 'It's over here!' So no, I didn't have an idea. Give me a break."

Honestly, he had expected to stand in the middle of the river and look carefully around him, scanning everything from the riverbed, to the banks of the river, to the space between the banks and the bottom of the cliffs, and finally to the cliffs themselves. It had to be pretty obvious, he thought, and if they didn't find the mark on the one side of the river, he and Jennifer would cross the river and check the other side.

He was also sure that Everett crashed the boat in a flood-stage river not far from his starting point next to the Rio Cebolla. Being on a flooded river, going through a narrow canyon in a small boat with more than a hundred pounds of dead weight in the bottom, Everett would have been in trouble from the moment he launched.

That meant Everett's mark should be close to where they started hiking. It's not like they would have to look along the whole canyon, so he didn't expect it to be so hard.

While there was far less water in the river than when they were rafting with Ted, the water still flowed at a good rate. Sometimes it was narrow and deep, sometimes broad and shallow, but always cold. Walking down the dry part of the riverbed wasn't so bad, but wading across it revealed deep pockets of water, slick rocks, and occasionally big boulders that had to be stepped around, all while the current pushed against their increasingly numb feet.

The stones of the riverbed were packed tight against each other like a badly made cobblestone street. They were rounded and crooked and uneven and covered in slick mud. Every step had to be taken with caution to keep from slipping and falling. When they wanted to get out of the riverbed, the banks were sometimes half as tall as they were, forcing them to scramble up on their knees and stomachs or wait until a boulder could be found that would allow them a step-up. Once on the bank, the grass was thick and high around large patches of sagebrush, making it a constant fight to find a good path.

Plodding farther from the riverbed and closer to the cliffs meant struggling through piñon and juniper trees, and around dense oak thickets. In areas where the cliffs came in and the canyon sides were steep, there was no bank at all, so they were left to slog their way through the mud and rocks.

On top of managing the physical difficulty was the constant attempt to distinguish any kind of mark that Everett might have left.

"Look at the rock walls for marks," Mogi said.

"Look for rocks piled on top of each other, like a cairn," Mogi said.

"Look for anything out of the ordinary," Mogi said.

But it was hard to see the rock faces of the canyon walls, much less what might be a man-made mark on them. Were they looking for letters, numbers, arrows, an X? There were a lot of rocks piled on top of each other, and not one of the piles was different from the last hundred they had seen. And besides, Jennifer wanted to know, just what does "ordinary" look like so that one could see anything "out" of it?

Two hot, tired, and irritated teen-agers finally sat down to eat lunch. The only thing cool was the silence between them.

"Okay, I was wrong," Mogi said after chewing his way through two dry sandwiches, hoping for a little sympathy from his sister.

She offered no words to console him.

"Okay, so I was stupid for even thinking that this would work," he added.

She again made no sound.

"Okay, so I was even stupider than usual, all right?"

He finally decided to just shut up, imagining that the situation couldn't get any worse.

That's when he saw a raindrop hit his daypack.

Jennifer looked up at the bottom of the dark clouds peeking over the rim of the canyon. "I don't suppose you remembered to bring any rain gear?"

Mogi didn't even bother looking up. It had just gotten worse.

"Oh, great," Jennifer said as the drops came bigger and faster. She put her sandwich wrapping and drink back into her daypack and balanced it on top of her head. "Let's find some shelter."

Mogi zipped up his pack, slipped it on, and trotted to catch up with her as she burrowed into a grove of trees. The splatter of the raindrops increased to machine-gun speed.

Sheltering under the trees worked for a few minutes, but soon the sky darkened even more, the clouds dipped below the rim of the canyon, and the water falling from them seemed like more than what was in the river. Soon, even the thick branches and pine needles were dripping on them.

"Okay!" Mogi yelled over the din of the tiny bombs landing around them. "We're done. Let's get out of here. We're going to be soaked no matter what, so we might as well be moving. I figure we've come halfway, so we maybe have three miles before we get to the monastery."

Jennifer shouldered her pack, pulled her cap down hard, and fell in line behind her brother as he stomped his way through the tall grass.

Some of the raindrops changed to hail. The little pieces of ice added a sting when they hit and made the air temperature plunge. It was hard to hear each other above the whapping of the drops on their caps and packs, so they hunkered down and silently trudged forward, shivering, with their shoulders hunched up against the wet.

In some places, the land along the river was wide, leaving an area open enough that they could walk quickly. In others, the cliffs moved in, narrowing the space for walking and slowing them down as they had to carefully pick their way through boulders and fallen branches.

The worst obstacles were the deep, mud-filled gullies that drained the rainwater cascading down the cliff faces. Years of rainfall had cut gullies several feet deep from the cliff bottoms through the banks all the way to the river. They could not be crossed at all, so the teens had to drop back onto the increasingly slick, dangerous, mud-covered stones in the riverbed.

After sliding down the bank and into the river to avoid the latest gully, their sneakers and clothing and their whole bodies were wet and muddy.

"Aaigh!" Mogi suddenly yelled as he slid against a large boulder in the middle of the river. He gripped what he could and fought the slide, but he was soon lying in the shallow water, his daypack submerged beneath him. He had stepped on a flat rock that shifted and tipped up beneath him. His foot slid back, jamming his ankle between the rock's edge and the boulder.

Stepping next to him, Jennifer slid her hands under his armpits to lift him up. But she slid on the river stones and lost her grip, unable to do anything to help her brother.

Getting his other leg bent and planted, Mogi raised his body as he fought the ankle that was pinned.

"Pull that rock out of the way!" he yelled, propping his upright leg against the boulder.

Jennifer shoved her hands into the foot-deep cold water, pulled and pushed, and finally shifted the rock out of its position. Mogi jerked his hurt ankle out of the water and fell back. Without words, Jennifer took his pack, slung it beside hers, and steadied him as he stood up and then bent over, using his hands to make a tripod as he hopped and shuffled his way to the bank.

Launching himself as much as he could up and onto the riverbank, Mogi rolled onto the grass as rain pelted his face.

He screamed.

CHAPTER

Jennifer struggled to get Mogi up, pulling on him, yelling at him, grabbing his belt to roll him off his back, doing whatever was needed to get him on his feet. Being on the riverbank in the tall grass in the rain was too exposed; she needed to get him back into the trees, up on sloped ground so he wouldn't end up in a pool of water.

The rain had let up, but the air was thick, wet, and cold, giving no relief as they lurched forward in their soaked clothing. Finally, after allowing his sister to pull him up and hustle him along, Mogi collapsed on a flat-topped boulder under the trees.

Jennifer carefully removed his shoe and pulled back the sock. Blood had soaked through the lower half; clearly the rock's edge had not only jammed against the ankle but sliced it open as well.

"Ow!" Mogi shouted through gritted teeth. The pain caused vomit to rise in his throat, and he did his best to spit and swallow until the taste left his mouth. Still feeling sick, he laid back on the rock, breathing fast and sweating, the drops of sweat feeling warmer against his wet fore-head. He began shivering.

"Don't lie down," Jennifer said, pulling him upright. "Let's get you wrapped up."

Though they didn't bring rain gear, each had stowed a hooded sweatshirt in their daypacks. Jennifer's was still largely dry, so she helped him out of his soaking T-shirt and forced the sweatshirt over his head. It was a tight fit, but with the wet, the cold, and now an injury, Jennifer knew she couldn't let him lose his body heat. She removed his wet cap and pulled the sweatshirt's hood tight around his face.

Unzipping the two packs, she dumped the contents on the ground and draped the packs over his quivering legs. The high-tech fabric was already beginning to dry.

"Listen to me," she said. "You have to stay warm, you understand?"

He nodded. He recognized the same dangers as she did—losing his heat would push him into hypothermia, where his body could no longer generate enough heat to keep his blood vessels open and blood flowing. His shiv-ering was already a bad sign.

Jennifer gathered the stuff that she had shook onto the ground and shoved it against the base of the rock—water bottles, empty food bags, three snack bars, and a plastic envelope that held Lisa Quintana's paper. At least, she thought, they were smart enough to put the paper in something that kept it from getting wet. She also found a large map of the Rio Chama canyon that Mogi had bor-rowed from Ted.

Leaning over the map to keep it as dry as possible, she unfolded and refolded the map until she could see the area between the Rio Cebolla and the monastery.

"Do you know where we are?" she asked, showing it to Mogi.

He wasn't feeling well, but was vastly warmer in the sweatshirt. Looking at the river, up and down the canyon, and then up at whatever parts of the rim he could see through the clouds, he tried to imagine the landscape they had passed.

It was the big cliff that he remembered. A large piece of the canyon wall came out from the side far enough that its base was actually in the river, beautifully colored with light browns and tans, with a white top. They had walked past it maybe fifteen minutes earlier.

He found it on the map and showed her. "We passed this. We must be in this area."

"Okay." Jennifer memorized the location, folded up the map, and stowed it inside her shirt. "I've got to go."

"You can't go. Please don't go. I want you to stay with me."

"You can't walk. You're crippled, and I can't carry you."

"You can't go!" Mogi cried.

"If I stay on this side of the canyon, I should reach the monastery in the next hour. I'll be back."

She stood, but Mogi grabbed her arm. "Don't leave me! Please!" he pleaded, his eyes tearing up. "Look, get me a tree branch that I can use as a crutch. All I need is a crutch and I'll be okay."

"You can't make it over this rough ground, and a crutch won't help you in the river. You just need to stay here until I get back. It should be a couple of hours at most."

He grabbed hold of her arm and lifted himself into a standing position. He folded up the leg with the hurt ankle so that it didn't touch the ground.

"Look, see? I can do this. All I need is a crutch. Look down the canyon—we're already out of the narrowest part, so we shouldn't need to cross the river anymore, and we're on the monastery side, so we should be only a couple of miles or so from their land. I can do this. Just get me a crutch."

Jennifer looked at the ground, torn by indecision. She shouldn't leave him unless there was no other way, and it would be better if he were moving rather than sitting.

"You bring a knife or something that I cut a piece of wood with?"

"Yup," Mogi said, reaching into his pocket and pulling out a large, wide-bladed folding knife. He handed it to her and sat back down. She moved into the trees, looking for an appropriate branch or stick.

There were several downed young trees with trunks that were only one or two inches in diameter. Finding one that looked sturdy enough, she levered the trunk against another tree and snapped it off so that a six-foot piece was left.

She brought it to her brother and had him stand up. "Do you want to hold it staff style, or should I cut it to fit your armpit?" she asked.

"Leave it long. I'll use both hands."

"We can use some cloth to pad it."

She hurriedly trimmed up the ragged end, cleaned the small branches and loose bark from the trunk, and tried to shave the upper end to make it smooth. Mogi took it, used his hands to position it, and then took several careful steps to see if it would work.

"This will do," he said, gritting his teeth against the pain exploding from his ankle. "Thanks. I can do this."

"Try not to fall over. You don't want to hurt your other leg."

She quickly gathered up their things and looked him in the eye. "But we have to move, right now."

They walked, carefully but aggressively, understanding the need to get to the car as quickly as possible.

Mogi struggled. He couldn't get comfortable with the crutch on the side of the hurt ankle, so he switched it to the other side. That didn't work any better, so he switched it back. Whatever side the crutch was on, he hopped with his good foot. Landing after the hop made his body jerk, which made his other leg jerk, which made his injured ankle jerk, which shot pains up and down his leg.

Both legs were beginning to cramp. His hands hurt against the raw wood of the crutch, and it occasionally slipped because it was still slick from the rain. He was cold and miserable.

"Uh-oh," he heard Jennifer say. He followed her gaze and his heart sank.

A few yards in front of them, at a particularly narrow part of the river, a deep gully ran from the cliffs all the way to the river. There was no way to go around it, and the sides were too steep to get down and then up. They had to go back into the riverbed.

It was no use discussing it. Jennifer chose the lowest point of the bank and lowered herself over the edge. It was only a two-foot drop, and once down, she positioned herself to help her brother.

Mogi sat close to the edge and then scooted himself over and down the gap, leaning his crutch in front of him and holding it as he swung his good foot off and onto the wet stones below. Jennifer grabbed his arm and pulled him toward her.

It wasn't pretty, but it worked.

They carefully stepped on the slick stones and sticky mud, eager to get back to the bank. Jennifer held Mogi as they gingerly stepped on or around the stones.

Halfway around the mouth of the gully, they heard a growling noise behind them. They stopped and looked back to see a wave of water, stretching from one side of the riverbank to the other, rushing toward them.

"They've released the water from the dam!" Mogi yelled. He started hurrying down the river, angling toward the bank in a panic—if they got caught in the wave, they'd be pushed over and dragged along.

Jennifer caught his arm, helping him to stay upright. He hopped as fast as he could, trying to avoid tripping on the stones or his crutch. It was only ten yards to the bank, but a pile of broken tree limbs forced them another ten yards down the river.

They moved harder, faster, as the sound grew behind them. Before they could reach the bank, the water rushed toward them and caught them behind their knees, buckling them and sweeping them into the current.

CHAPTER

13

Mogi lost his grip on his crutch and watched it shoot into the wave just before his head was sucked under. He thrashed his arms and tried to keep his hurt ankle from banging against the bottom. Then Jennifer was grabbing his hand. Using his good foot, he pushed hard against the river stones, hard again and again, lunging his body out of the water and toward the bank. Jennifer flailed against the water and did her own lunging to escape the water's pull.

Though it seemed longer, no more than thirty seconds had passed from the time the wave hit to when they were throwing themselves up the bank and out of the water. Their chests were heaving, their hands and arms shaking, their legs numb from the churning water.

Mogi's ankle was killing him, and the rest of his body felt like it had been savagely beaten. He was shaking so much he couldn't focus on what Jennifer was saying.

"Get your shirt off!" Jennifer yelled into his ear, loud enough that he jerked his head away. She pulled at the sweatshirt. Nothing was dry now; everything was soaked.

The sun broke through the clouds, and it was an immediate relief to feel the warm sunlight on their skin.

Jennifer was up wringing first her T-shirt, then the sweatshirt he'd been wearing, folding and refolding, squeezing out as much water as she could, and at the same time pounding her feet against the ground to get some feeling back and to stop her own shivering.

Having done as much as she could, she pulled Mogi to an upright position, found a flat boulder in the open, and laid him back against it. Again she laid the quickly drying backpacks over his shivering skin.

"Stay in the sun, okay?

Mogi was confused. The sun felt good, but what did she say?

"How far have we come since we started?"

What was she talking about?

Jennifer yelled at her brother. "How much farther to go!"

Mogi wasn't thinking straight. He had no idea what she wanted from him.

Jennifer leaned close to his face and made him look into her eyes. "I have to go. There's no other choice. I will be back as soon as I can."

He couldn't muster much resistance but weakly grabbed her hand. She pulled away from him and started walking, not looking back. She didn't want to leave but knew that finding help was their only chance of getting out of this mess.

She began to run.

She ran as carefully as she could, watching the ground in front of her, avoiding the cactus and thorny bushes, leaping over downed trees, glancing up in front of her to reckon her path. She needed ten yards. Then ten yards more. Then another ten.

The riverbank was wide, and she found no more large gullies pushing her into the river; the small ones she jumped across. The ground was mainly grass, but the trees sometimes reached to the bank, and she had to thread her way through, dodging trunks and bushes, but always running. Running as deliberately as she could, running like she was late for something important.

Sniffing back tears, she came out of a stand of thin, raggedy pine trees and suddenly stopped.

There was a man with an umbrella.

Shocked to see anyone at all, her first reaction was surprise at seeing an umbrella. It was not an ordinary umbrella, but an extra large one of bright yellow, blue, and red. The colors glared against the gray, brown, and muted green of the surroundings.

Golf, she thought. It was a monster umbrella like golfers carry with them.

The man lifted the umbrella above him, swept it to the side, and let it drop to the ground.

He was a monk. His habit—a full-length, heavy, hooded robe with a rope belt—hung from his shoulders. The hem around the bottom had been gathered at four points, pulled up, and tucked under the belt, revealing a set of long, white, muscular legs.

Jennifer suddenly shook with urgency but uttered no sound, stunned by her surprise.

The monk started laughing. Not a small, joking laugh; not a chuckle; not a breathy, mild laugh. This man had spread his arms wide apart, looked upward, closed his eyes, and laughed loud, strong, and long. It was a laugh of delight and glee, like a man who was thrilled and overcome with happiness.

A laugh of pleasure and awe.

"Help," Jennifer finally said in a meek voice. "Help!" she said louder as she stumbled toward him.

If the man was startled or surprised, he gave no indication. He turned to her, lowered his hood behind his head, and began striding toward her.

Jennifer cried as she stumbled through a description of what had happened, pointing the way back and then hurrying next to the man, working to keep up with his long strides. He was taller than he had looked in the distance; she was surprised at how big he was—broad shoulders, muscled calves, big feet in big sandals, and a large head.

*　*　*

Mogi casually watched as Jennifer left him. There was enough pain filling his body that he didn't even wonder where she was going.

The sun felt good, and there was no breeze. He shifted against the hard points of the rock, trying to get every bit of sunlight on his skin. Breathing deeply, he brushed beads of water from his face, then his chest. He couldn't feel his legs beyond the throbbing of his ankle.

Is this how Everett Cossey felt?

Mogi imagined being in an old-time boat—small, short, wobbly in the water, probably leaky to begin with—and thought of what Everett experienced. Soaked to the skin from water that had only days before been snow and ice, Everett would have been cold, wet, and filled with desperation. Afraid, yes, probably scared completely out of his mind. Worried about Orin, and worried about the gold.

Everett would have left the gold and focused on surviving, but Orin, yeah, Orin wouldn't have liked that. He would have yelled at him, cursed him, beat him. Beat him like a dog.

Mogi shivered, a chill crossing his chest as the sun went behind a cloud. He felt around for the sweatshirt and pulled it across him. It was damp, but the pressure against his skin made him feel better.

Hey!

Mogi started. What?

Hey!

Mogi looked where Jennifer had gone. A man stood past the grass, up near the trees. He had no shirt on, his skin white against the shadows around him. He was shivering violently, rubbing his arms, hopping up and down, bending over, obviously trying to get some kind of warmth going in his arms and legs.

The man looked at Mogi and raised a shivering hand as if he were anxious for a friend.

A friend.

They both would have given all that gold for a friend.

*　　*　　*

Mogi was where she had left him, her sweatshirt wadded up on top of his chest. His eyes were closed as if in hard concentration, and he shivered violently as they knelt next to him.

His eyes opened when he felt hands on his skin but he gave no response or resistance. He was too cold for anything to matter. The large man touching him said nothing but quickly looked into Mogi's eyes, felt his pulse, and ran his hands over the swollen, blackened ankle.

Without comment, he lifted Mogi upright and then folded him across his shoulders with hardly an effort. He nodded toward the daypacks and their contents on the ground. Jennifer immediately gathered up everything, stuffing it quickly into the packs, and then zipped them tight. She hurried to catch up to the monk who was already yards ahead of her.

CHAPTER
14

Mogi wondered if he had fallen asleep. He remembered being carried for what seemed like a long time, but now he was lying on some kind of sleeping pallet on a floor.

He looked around the room. It was a rustic, cabin-like room, really small, not much larger than his bedroom at home. It had almost no furnishings—a roaring propane heater, a table and chair, a fully packed bookshelf, a blanket-covered mattress that lay on a platform hanging by chains from a wall, and another platform with legs that held a small sink with the plumbing exposed below it. A floor-to-ceiling curtain hung in front of a smaller room in the corner, which he assumed was a closet, or maybe a bathroom.

Everything was wood. Wood floors, wood walls, a pitched ceiling of pine boards. Even the shelves were held up by pieces of lumber carved in various shapes and figures. Everything appeared to be handmade.

The important thing was that it was warm—too warm. He sighed deeply and threw back the blanket to find that his clothes had been replaced with sweatpants and a large sweatshirt.

"Hey."

Jennifer stepped out from the room behind the curtain, a flushing sound confirming it was a bathroom. She sat on the bed, rubbing her hair with a towel. She had on billowing sweatpants pulled high and a sweatshirt that hung to her knees.

Mogi tried to stretch and was quickly reminded of why he was on the floor. His ankle was throbbing.

He raised himself up on one elbow and looked down. His ankle had been wrapped with an elastic bandage, something else he didn't remember.

"Where are we?"

"This is the very humble home of Brother Sebastian," Jennifer said. "He's a monk with the monastery. He's off telling the abbot about us and should be back soon."

Mogi lay back, thinking, trying to remember.

"What happened? All I remember is that my ankle hurt really bad and I was wet and cold."

"Brother Sebastian happened to be out walking in the rain when I was hiking back to the monastery. I led him back to you, and he carried you here. This cabin is about a mile closer to where I left you than the monastery itself, so we were able to stop here and get you warm, let you rest a bit. It was incredibly fortunate that he was there, and so willing to help."

"Jeez," Mogi said. "Thank you."

"You're welcome, but we're both under God's grace in this one. I could probably have made it on my own to find help at the monastery, but it would have taken a lot longer to get back to you. You were really cold, by the way."

They were quiet for a few moments.

"I'd like to get up," Mogi said, shifting his body. He rose and scooted across the floor to the bed. Carefully planting his good leg and letting Jennifer help him, he half-stood, rocked forward and back, and then sat down on the mattress. He found the sitting position to be easier on his back, but it sent waves of pain through his leg as the blood sank into his ankle. He grimaced.

They heard footsteps outside, and the door opened. A large man in a monk's robe came in and closed the door behind him.

Wow, Mogi thought. He must be six-five, or six-six. Lean, for sure, but his head, hands, and feet are huge. Another fifty pounds and he could be an NFL lineman.

The man walked over to the bed, felt Mogi's forehead and pulse, looked in his eyes, knelt down, and then ran his hands over the swollen ankle. "How does it feel?" His voice was deep, with a soft, comforting tone.

"Uh, it hurts."

Brother Sebastian smiled, showing a row of white, straight teeth. "I bet it does. You're going to have to go to the emergency room and let them stitch up that cut. I put tape across it, but you need stitches."

"Thank you," Mogi stammered.

"You can thank your sister. She's a very determined young woman. Without her, things would have been much worse."

Brother Sebastian turned, took a teapot from a shelf, filled it with water from a plastic jug, lit a burner on the propane stove, and placed the pot on top. He turned off the heater, rolled up the sleeping pallet, and stood it against a wall.

"A little hot tea will do us all wonders," he said, rubbing his hands together. "It warms not only the body but the soul."

He turned the chair to face them and sat down. "I am called Brother Sebastian, but you may call me Brother Sebastian." He let out a huge belly laugh. Then he smiled. "Welcome to my home."

Jennifer was smiling, having already had some time to get used to the strange monk. Mogi was flustered, not knowing how to respond to a monk who seemed, well, so happy. Weren't monks supposed to be sad and suffering?

"Thank you," he said. "I'm very grateful to be here."

"What were you doing in the canyon?"

"Oh, uh, we—"

"We were trying to find the stolen gold," Jennifer admitted. She slid off the bed and picked up a backpack, unzipping it quickly to pull out the plastic-covered story about the robbery. She showed the title to the monk.

"Ah, the famous stolen gold," Brother Sebastian said. "Did you find it?"

Mogi's face turned red. "Uh, no," he murmured.

"One of us thought," Jennifer began, elbowing her brother, "that the guy who hid the gold would have left a mark someplace to show where he hid it. We thought that maybe we could find the mark."

Brother Sebastian smiled. "A mark that would last a hundred and thirty years would be a good mark indeed. Did you find one?"

"No, again," Mogi said, remembering to feel stupid.

"Ah, well. Perhaps you were meant to find a different treasure."

"But we need the money now," Mogi said. "I mean, you guys, uh, the brothers, uh, the monastery, need the money right now."

Brother Sebastian's face filled with surprise. "I didn't know. Do we need money?"

For the next few minutes, Mogi blurted his way through their coming to Ghost Ranch, the raft trip, Sheila Winters, her business in California, the land across from the monastery, the mineral pool Ted had found, the potential geothermal electrical plant, and the need for the monastery to get a lawyer as quickly as possible.

"Hmm," Brother Sebastian finally responded. "That's quite a story. And you say that your mother is a writer. Based on you two, I bet she's a really good one. Ghost Ranch is lucky to have her."

A gurgling whistle brought him to his feet. He set out three mugs, added teabags, and poured water into each one. He passed a mug to each of his visitors, set his on the table, and sat down again.

Mogi couldn't think of what to say next. It was like Brother Sebastian hadn't heard a thing. "But you have to fight this," Mogi continued. "It could mean the ruin of the monastery if you don't."

"Hmm," Brother Sebastian uttered again. "I could give you a platitude like, 'Oh, God will take care of everything,' but I'm not a big believer in platitudes. It usually means that someone doesn't have a good answer to a good question. In this case, however, we've already been involved. The land was even offered to us before Ms. Winters gave her offer."

Mogi was surprised. "You didn't take it?"

"We didn't need the land. God blesses us with all we need. It also cost a good deal of money that we didn't have. Mr. Archuleta, the owner of the land, is in a desperate situation because of his wife. The problems with her dementia came quicker than expected, and he's facing expenses of a care facility, doctors, medicine, and more, as well as paying off the ranch debts incurred during the years of drought. He would have much preferred to sell the land to the monastery but couldn't drop the price. Sheila's offer, I expect, is a Godsend for him."

"But. . .but keeping the electrical generation plant from being built is really important."

"I didn't say it wasn't. But many things are important. We'll be watching. Many things have to happen for this to be successful, and there may be better ways to address our concerns. Meanwhile, can I ask a favor?"

Both Mogi and Jennifer were surprised. What could he possibly want?

"Uh, sure."

"Can I see the story about the gold?"

Jennifer passed him the research paper. Brother Sebastian laughed with glee, rubbed his hands together, and was immediately absorbed in the story of the robbery. Within five minutes, he had leafed through every page.

"What fun!" he said with a laugh. "I've heard about the mystery of the robbery for years but have never read all the facts. Whoever wrote this paper is a good writer. And the map! I finally get to see the map." It was as if the monk had been given a Christmas present.

He removed the staple from the papers and held the photocopy of the map closer to the light. Then he quickly put the map on the desk, took a pencil, and began tracing the lines that represented the river and its canyon.

Jennifer and Mogi watched with interest as Brother Sebastian made several marks on the map.

"The turn here is sharper," he said as he broadened the river line a little. "And there's a side canyon that belongs here. Oh, I know this place—it's farther down than this, there's a split channel here, and. . . ."

With every comment, Brother Sebastian added more lines or fattened lines or added little comments in the empty area of the paper. He was clearly absorbed in making the map more accurate. He suddenly looked up, his face flushing red. "Oh, I'm sorry. I've walked this canyon for a lot of years. I know it by heart. It has become a part of me, and to see something not quite right makes me want to correct it. Have you solved the mystery of the man who was shot and stabbed?"

This guy was something else, Mogi was thinking. This isn't how a monk is supposed to act, is it? I mean, he should be solemn, and prayerful, and chant a lot. Isn't he supposed to be grim? Is it appropriate for him to be enthused about ghost stories? Don't monks read only scripture?

"Uh, well, I'm still working on it," Mogi said, "but Jennifer figured out the important stuff. It's all in understanding the two brothers."

The three talked, Mogi reviewing his ideas of what did or did not happen, Jennifer explaining her ideas of the brothers, and Brother Sebastian asking questions and making observations.

"You can keep this stuff if you want it," Mogi said, lifting his foot. "It looks like we're out of the treasure hunting business for a while."

Brother Sebastian smiled. "I am honored."

"Can I ask you a question?" Jennifer said suddenly.

"Of course."

"Are you sure you're a monk?" she asked.

Brother Sebastian roared with laughter, his cheeks growing red and tears coming to his eyes. It took several seconds for him to catch his breath.

"Oh, dear," he said, wiping his eyes. "I'll have to remember to tell that one to the abbot."

He smiled.

"Yes, I am a monk. This lifestyle I have chosen best suits how I serve God. I am not, however, of the Benedictine Order, as are the brothers of the monastery. I asked to be here and was granted a special arrangement. I participate in most of what the brothers do, but I have different gifts that permit me to be, uh, somewhat irregular with my daily schedule."

"But you don't seem like a monk," Mogi added. "When we visited the monastery on our rafting trip, everybody we saw looked . . . uh . . . sad, or penitent, like they felt bad."

Brother Sebastian nodded in agreement. "They really aren't, but I understand why you would see them that way. If you could see them in all the things they do, you would find them happy and bright and joyful, and very active. Everyone here loves being here, and there's lots of laughter at certain times. It is a very, very special place, and do not doubt that everyone here is passionately in love with God and devoted to the monastic life.

"But I can see why you have a different idea of a monk's life. It's a common perception that monks lead lives of suffering and punishment, whipping ourselves, crawling around on our knees, forever asking forgiveness for our sins, and that we never actually do anything.

"But let me respond about myself. I am a monk but, perhaps, not the usual model of one. I laugh. I sing at the top of my voice. I stand outside in rainstorms, swim in the river without the benefit of clothes, and eat a little meat. If I look happy, it is because I am happy. My life experiences have given me a somewhat different take on a life of sincere devotion. God has given me the gift of being a writer, and I teach others by writing about my experiences. That is why I'm content to be alone in my humble cottage.

"I'm sure the abbot is secretly happy that I don't join the others very often at their regular meals, which are eaten in silence. He knows that I'd break out laughing or something and ruin the whole thing!" He laughed again.

There were sounds of machines outside and a knock on the door.

"Ah," Brother Sebastian said. "That must be your transportation." He opened the door and greeted two men in similar robes.

As Jennifer helped Mogi stand up, he glanced out the open door.

"Monks ride ATVs?" he said in astonishment.

The extra-large monk grinned. "Faster than crawling on our knees!"

Jennifer chuckled and began gathering up their things.

"Before you go," Brother Sebastian said. "Let me at least give you your map back. I can get another one, and if you return to your treasure hunting, perhaps the details I've added will help guide you."

He went to the table, folded the map, unfolded it, and then folded it again along different lines. "Well, I was trying to fold it along the creases of the original map so that it wouldn't mess up the lines I added, but I can't seem to figure out which of the existing creases to use."

Mogi hopped over to the table, looked at what Brother Sebastian had done, and folded it himself. Then he unfolded it and laid the map flat on the table. He stared at it, not saying a word, for a full minute.

Brother Sebastian glanced questioningly at Jennifer. She stood still, watching and wondering.

Mogi finally stood up straight, turned to the others, and said, "Everett Cossey was a lot smarter than we gave him credit for."

CHAPTER
15

In the deep canyon of the Rio Chama
May 19, 1882

Everett Cossey was spread-eagle across the small boat, his hands tightly gripping the sides and his legs spread wide across the floor to fight the threat of tipping over. Shifting his weight as much as he could to keep the boat under some kind of control, he held on as he was jerked and jolted by the river's flooding waters. Rock walls, trees along the riverbank, overhanging cliffs, boulders the size of houses, fat thickets of spiny brush, and mounds of undercut dirt—it all raced by. Everett feared that at any moment some catastrophe would dump him into the raging water.

Then, as if determined to do itself the most harm, the boat smashed into the top of a mostly submerged boulder, bowed as it tried to peel itself off, and then gave a pitiful moan as it spun and tore itself loose. Through a newly opened seam, a stream of water now gushed around Everett's feet. Then, with a sudden pop, a board splintered and water spouted up like the blowhole of a whale.

Everett panicked. He could not, could not, could not lose the gold. Grabbing the rope tied in back, he watched for a clear portion of riverbank ahead of him, waited until the boat was shoved in its direction, and jumped.

He hit above the rim of the bank and stumbled onto the grass. He rolled over as the rope tightened, digging in his heels, and fought against the river to keep the boat from being swept away. He edged it closer into a shallow place on the shore as it slowly filled with water. Everett strained to get his end up on the tiny patch of ground until the river finally yielded and quit the battle, leaving the boat half in, half out of the water. Everett had won.

He fell back in exhaustion. That he lay on solid ground, that he was no longer at the mercy of the water, was a glorious feeling. He allowed himself a smile that lasted only a moment before he remembered his situation.

Orin was going to beat him good.

It wasn't often that Orin's rage came out. Someplace in his brother's soul, someplace dark and remote, there was a viciousness that sometimes escaped. When it did, Everett had learned that running was not a shameful act. Too often, he did not run fast enough and Orin would beat him, whip him, grind him until pain rendered him unconscious. He knew that Orin didn't mean it, that it was a demon he could not control, and that he would be sorrowful afterward, but it was little comfort when Orin raged over him.

The cold finally got Everett off the ground. His pants were soaked, and his legs numb. Fighting chills, he knew he had to empty the boat. It sat jammed into the ground, but if a large wave twisted it more, the boat might swivel, tip, and dump the gold into the water.

Struggling in the muddy water, Everett leaned into the boat, grabbed a bag, pulled it up and over the side, and then swung it some feet onto the bank. It was hard, back-breaking work and wearying to an already exhausted man. He repeated the grueling task over and over until the boat was finally empty.

Once done, Everett pulled off his socks and boots and stood still as his pants drained water. There was enough daylight peeking over the tops of the canyon walls to give him some warmth, and he stood gratefully in the sunshine.

Now what?

He was never meant to bury the gold. It was what the plan had said and what everybody was told, but there was another plan—a second plan known only to him and Orin.

Orin never intended to split the gold among the others and considered them fools for not realizing it. That made it *their* fault that they would find themselves cheated.

The second plan, the real one, had Everett not stopping but rowing the boat through the canyon to where Orin would be waiting on the other side. Escaping the sheriff and his posse, Orin would have left a trail like he was going west when he really had dropped into a small ar-royo taking him south to the Rio Gallina. He would fol-low a steep trail down that canyon and ride back to the Chama where the two brothers would meet, fill their sad-dlebags full of gold, and ride lickety-split for Mexico, or maybe California. Forget about the others.

His breath returning, his panic seeping away, Everett unrolled the map and slid it from its oilskin cover. He studied the lines Orin had drawn showing the canyon rim and the river. Where was he? He needed to know where he was so he could tell Orin.

When the two brothers explored the canyon in February, there was one sandstone cliff along the rim that was different from the others. It was as tall as the tallest cliffs along the edge, but came out from the canyon walls. Almost straight up and down, its smooth sides ran from the high rim to the very bottom where its base was buried in the river itself. Orin had used that solitary cliff as a landmark and had decided to put the X a hundred yards upriver from it. That X was used to fool the others.

Today, shivering in the sunlight, it was that actual cliff that Everett was looking at. He had landed not forty feet from its base.

He traced the lines of the map carefully, looking up at the cliff and confirming that he was right. Everett was finally happy—he could bury the gold here and be able to tell Orin exactly where it was. Things hadn't gone the way of the plan, but now he'd do something smart that would please his big brother. They'd have to come back, but at least the gold would be safe until then.

Everett took a deep breath, wrung his socks out again, and strained to pull on his soaked boots. Orin was waiting for him, and he wouldn't tolerate Everett being lazy when the law was after them, so it was best that he get to work. He had to hide the gold, fix the boat, and get on down the river.

The shovel stowed in the boat had been lost overboard, so he looked for boulders small enough to roll up and throw the bags under, but he found none that would budge. He looked for fallen trees that had left a hole from their roots, but none were bigger than a single bag. He thought about emptying the bags into the middle of a large oak thicket, but worried that the shiny coins would be seen.

He looked around frantically. If he couldn't bury the gold, then he had to hide it behind something. His panic returning, he shivered with frustration and cold, looking everywhere, straining to see anything that could serve as a hiding place. Breaks in the riverbed? Gullies cutting through the landscape? Logs that could be rolled on top of the bags?

He was growing desperate, but then he noticed it.

On that big towering cliff of solid sandstone, the one that went from the water all the way to the rim, there was a break in the rock's surface. About fifteen feet off the ground, a portion of the cliff had split away from the face, a flat slab that now leaned at an angle away from the wall, revealing a large crack behind it.

A perfect hiding place.

All Everett had to do was get the bags up to that crack and throw them in. They would be completely hidden from sight. Even if someone came along looking for the gold, they would never guess that the bags were hidden above them.

Over the next hour, Everett moved the bags directly below the split rock and dragged over four saplings that had fallen. He used the rope from the boat to bind the small trunks together, making knots every foot along their length. When he was done, he stood the bundle of trunks on end, having created a crude but workable ladder with the top extending just over the beginning of the crack between the fallen slab and the cliff.

He shouldered each bag up as far as he could, far enough that he could then pitch them into the crack. His muscles soon felt stretched and useless, but he worked with urgency. He had to get back to Orin.

After throwing in the final bag, Everett climbed down and dismantled his ladder. He dragged the saplings back into the woods, wiping away his tracks as he went. He coiled the rope and placed it next to the boat.

The boat, without the gold in the bottom, was now easy to drag farther up the riverbank. He turned it upside down, wrapped his shirt around the shattered boards, and stuffed what he could into the cracks, using a rock to pound them back into place.

He was ready.

One more thing, he thought. It wouldn't matter that Everett could remember exactly what he did and exactly where he did it and could bring Orin to the exact hiding spot—Orin wouldn't trust him.

He needed to mark the map.

Everett really, really needed a pen or a pencil, but he had nothing. It was a hard problem, and he fretted over it, pushed by the lengthening shadows inside the canyon.

Then it came to him. Simple, exact, permanent, and it wouldn't be seen by anyone even though they stared right at it.

I'm not as dumb as Orin thinks!

Everett rolled the map along a bottom board of the boat, located the cliff and where it split, folded the paper in one direction, and used his fingernail to make a hard crease right through the tall cliff. He made a similar crease in a different direction such that the two creases crossed directly above the gold's location. The two creases were obvious to him and the crossing exact, but they were objectively no different from the other creases in the paper. If a person didn't know which ones to pay attention to, he or she would never know that those two creases told a story that the others did not.

Everett was proud. This would do fine, he thought. Just fine. Momma would be proud of him, and even Orin might be impressed.

He slid the map into the oilskin, rolled it, tucked it back under his belt, turned the boat over, and shoved it back into the fast current.

He forgot the rope.

Without the heavy gold in the bottom, the boat acted like a bobbing cork, immediately spinning out of control. Lying spread-eagle across the boat was okay when the gold was in the bottom, but was *not* okay without it. The boat was thrown violently from one crashing wave to the next. Everett shifted and leaned and moved and fought it bravely for most of an hour until, utterly exhausted, he leaned over too far. His hand slipped and he fell against the side, dipping the edge into a large wave that swamped the boat completely, flipping it over and throwing him into the freezing water.

He was swallowed by the brown swirls and sucked to the bottom of the river.

He never came up.

CHAPTER
16

Mogi fluffed up the pillow under his knee and wished, for the umpteenth time, that Ghost Ranch had internet access. Even cell service would be nice. He understood the desire to provide a simple, rustic retreat for its guests, but he wasn't used to being so disconnected from everything.

After leaving Brother Sebastian's cabin on Friday afternoon, he and Jennifer were taken to an infirmary in the back part of the monastery complex. While an elderly monk checked his injured ankle and rewrapped the bandage, Jennifer called her mom, explained the situation, and arranged to pick her up so they could all drive to the hospital in Española, more than an hour away.

The news was not good. A torn ligament in Mogi's ankle would require surgery. He was given a stiff boot to wear until Monday, allowing time for the swelling to go down before the operation. Until then, he had to stay off his foot.

Which was okay with his mother. Being confined to the casita for the weekend would serve as punishment for being a little too "free spirited" and ignoring the risks he should have recognized. He could suffer in their casita alone while she and Jennifer went to museums and art galleries in Santa Fe.

Now it was Sunday, and Mogi, bored to death on the couch, continued to rest his foot. Jennifer was working in the ranch kitchen while his mom was out on one of the ranch's van tours.

In the mid-afternoon, there was a knock on the door. As much as Mogi would have liked to open it himself, he called out instead for the visitor to come in.

When the door opened, he was so shocked he forgot to breathe. It was Sheila Winters.

"Well, there's a cowboy who's not going to be on a horse for a while," she said. She came in, stood at the end of the couch as they exchanged greetings, and then pulled up the desk chair and sat down.

"I hear you found the famous treasure," she said. "I thought I would stop by and congratulate you."

Mogi was stunned. How in the world did she find out?

"Uh, I haven't actually found anything."

Of course, Mogi had been ready to immediately go find the treasure, but trying to put weight on his ankle demonstrated the foolishness of that idea. Going any-where apart from the hospital would have to wait.

"Oh, I thought you had. You did discover the secret to the map though, right?"

No one but Jennifer and Brother Sebastian knew what Mogi had discovered as he folded and refolded the map, right? He had shown them where the creases crossed and, looking closely at the other creases in the paper, knew that it was not accidental; it had to be Everett's method of marking the location of the gold.

Who else might have heard about it? Mogi tried to remember whom he had spoken to.

The two monks who had driven the ATVs were there when he passed the map to Jennifer and Brother Sebastian, showing the discovery.

He sort of remembered telling the doctor at the hospital about the adventure. And the nurses. Did he show them the map? Well, yeah, since it was in his pocket.

How about at Ghost Ranch when they got back? A number of people from his mom's class had come to check on him and they got to chatting, and—shoot!

He'd had a fine time describing the canyon and the river and his injury and the rescue and how he discovered the creases and what they meant and he even showed them the map—the whole bunch of them! He had gotten carried away and become a regular fount of information.

Dummy, dummy, dummy! Someone must have talked to Sheila.

"Uh, well, not exactly," he said cautiously. "I think I have an idea, but I won't really know until I go look."

"Well, from what I hear, it's a pretty good bet. I'm really impressed that someone as young and uneducated as you would be able to make such a good guess."

Mogi didn't find that to be a compliment, especially the "uneducated" part, and he certainly hadn't "guessed."

"I was trying to imagine," Sheila continued, "how much a hundred and fifty pounds of gold would be worth. If I remember from the news last night, gold is about $1,200 an ounce. A hundred and fifty, times sixteen, is 2,400 ounces. So, if the gold were to be found, it would be worth almost $3 million."

She smiled.

"Which, unfortunately, isn't *really* a lot of money. For example, the land I bought last week? Three million wouldn't even cover half. I'm not sure if you pay attention to such things, but land prices always go up, so if I ever had an idea of selling it, oh, to a company or to the monastery, for example, I'm sure that the price would be a lot more than what I paid for it. That means that having $3 million wouldn't make a difference, which makes finding the gold rather unimportant."

She rose from the chair, pushed it back to the desk, and opened the door.

"Get well, now." She smiled briefly and closed the door behind her.

Mogi sat, stunned, for several moments. Did she just tell him that, even if the monastery did have the gold, it wouldn't be enough to buy the land?

Wait a minute. Nobody had said anything about buying the land; the monastery had already turned down the chance to make an offer. That's not what she was telling him.

She was telling him that he shouldn't waste his time looking any further for the gold.

Which is exactly what one gold hunter would tell another gold hunter.

Mogi gritted his teeth from the pain as he peg-legged himself to the corral, the boot pounding the dirt.

"Ted! Ted!" he yelled as he swung open the gate and hobbled into the barn.

Ted seemed as casual and relaxed as ever as he came out of a back room to greet Mogi.

"Sheila Winters is going after the gold!" Mogi yelled.

* * *

"Well, you can't really blame him," Jennifer said after listening to her brother rant for longer than she wanted to listen. "He's got obligations, schedules, duties. He can't drop everything to run over to the river and spend hours searching for something that hasn't been found for more than a century even if you think you know exactly where it is."

"You think he doesn't believe me?" Mogi asked.

Jennifer looked her brother straight in the eye. "I don't even believe you, but though I haven't believed you in the past, you have delivered some amazing solutions to unsolved problems, so I'm willing to give you the benefit of the doubt. Ted is not. And, by the way, stumping around in a cast that you earned from your last wrong guess doesn't exactly support your cause."

Mogi slumped on the bed, accepting the painful truth that his connections between the map, the creases, and the secret hiding place looked pretty thin, regardless of how convinced he was that it all fit together. He had, indeed, wanted Ted to drop everything and race back to the river to find the spot where the two creases crossed.

But Ted had a trail ride that evening and was moving horses to a different pasture on Monday. Besides, a several-mile hike down the Chama wasn't exactly a lunchtime outing. He couldn't abandon his work, no matter how sure Mogi felt about his latest clue.

As Jennifer got ready for bed, Mogi continued to moan and fret and feel disgusted. He was sure that it was the lowest point of his life.

First, he and Jennifer had figured out that Sheila Winters was intending to ruin the valley by building an industrial plant.

Second, to get enough money to fight against the powers of evil that she represented, he had led Jennifer into the canyon on a search that had almost killed him.

Third, he figured out the secret of the map and then, in a brilliant show of stupidity, broadcast the location to the very person intent on ruining the valley in the first place.

He could see Sheila Winters dancing her way through the forest, finding a heaping pile of gleaming gold coins, rolling in them, throwing them in the air with glee, and carrying bucketloads of it out of the canyon. Now she would be even better equipped to destroy everything that the remote river canyon stood for.

Mogi didn't sleep much that night.

CHAPTER

17

Jennifer turned to close the door but found her brother limping through it.

"Uh, you know, this is supposed to be a private moment," she said as he softly closed the door behind her.

They were in the casita's only bathroom. It was 3 o'clock in the morning. Their mother was asleep in the next room.

"You've got to go after the gold," Mogi said as he quietly moved past her, placing both hands on the bathtub to lower himself onto the closed toilet seat, painfully extending his leg with the walking boot.

"Do you mind?" Jennifer hissed. "This is a bathroom. I prefer to be alone in the bathroom."

"Use it later," Mogi said, ignoring the urgency in her hiss. "I'm not going to have a chance to talk to you before we leave for the hospital, so you've got to listen to me now. I can't go after the gold, so you have to do it. I'm betting that Sheila Winters will make her move today, so you have to go as soon as possible."

"Uh, let's see. What day is it? Oh, yeah. It's Monday, the day that *all three of us* go to the hospital for *your* surgery."

"Forget about me. I'll do perfectly fine without you. I don't know how you're going to get out of it, but make something up. The important thing is that *you* have to do it. Go to the place that's marked on the map and get the gold."

"Okay, wonder boy, just how am I supposed to do that? I am *not* going to walk the river again. I am *not* going to wander through the private Benedictine monastery with monks who believe their devotion to God is enhanced by being *alone*. And I *can't* fly. Any other suggestions?"

Mogi's eyes, red and puffy from lack of sleep, looked into his sister's face with resigned desperation.

"I don't know *how* you're going to do it," he pleaded, "but you *have* to find a way. You *have* to go. If Sheila Winter gets the gold, nothing will stop her. Only by beating her to it is this mess going to get any better."

*　*　*

How long do they pray and sing?

Jennifer couldn't remember what the guestmaster had said, but she was pretty sure the monks met first before daylight, then had breakfast, and then met for something or other until eight or nine, after which they started their work for the day.

She was standing before the tall, thick, closed doors of the chapel by eight o'clock, but she wasn't about to knock or ring the bell. She would wait until they came out.

All three Franklins had arrived at the hospital for Mogi's check-in at 7 o'clock. His surgery was scheduled for 10:15, and he would be released in the late afternoon. Not having anything to do until the surgery, Jennifer told her mom that she needed to return the sweatpants and sweatshirts to Brother Sebastian.

She'd run them right up there and be back in a flash.

She hated to lie to her mother, hated it like crazy, but she couldn't figure out anything else to do.

The big doors opened, and a line of hooded monks silently passed into the bright sunshine.

It wasn't hard to find Brother Sebastian in the crowd since he was a head taller than most of the other monks. His eyes twinkled when he saw her, he motioned for her to be silent, and then they walked down the path to the cottonwoods next to the river. It wasn't until they were seated on a rustic bench that he pulled back his hood and was ready to listen.

She quickly ran through the happenings since Friday afternoon, including Sheila Winters' visit on Sunday, and ended with the middle-of-the-night session in the bathroom.

"I am so truly sorry to disturb you," she continued, standing up. "But I don't know, I just . . . I can't. . . ." She took a deep breath and let it out slowly. "I can't do this without help."

She flopped back down on the bench.

"What do you think your brother fears most?" Brother Sebastian asked.

Jennifer was surprised by the question. "Well, I think Sheila Winters' building the generating plant and ruining the monastery and the entire valley is number one."

"I don't think so," he said. "Guess again."

Jennifer didn't understand what he was asking for. "It's got to be Sheila Winters finding the gold."

"Um, nope, I don't think so."

She shook her head. "Uh, there're so many things to consider. . . ."

"Let me propose an answer," the monk said. "Your brother is pretty special, right? You told me about some of your adventures. Maybe he's even gifted in his ability to solve puzzles and mysteries?"

"Oh, yeah. Definitely."

"Then I would guess that what he fears most is being wrong. In this case, he's worried that the gold isn't where he said it is. And it's especially bad for him since he advertised it to several people, and many people think he might even be right. If it's not where he says it is, then he didn't solve the robbery, didn't solve what happened in the canyon with Everett, and was wrong about the map. On top of his foolishness in the canyon last week, he'd feel like a fool all the way around, and everybody would know it."

"Oh, yeah," Jennifer said, slumping like her bones were loose. "He'd be devastated. He takes everything really personally."

"So, even though he has good intentions toward the monastery and the canyon, talks about his good intentions toward the monastery and the canyon, and wants justice to win over evil, he still really wants to be right."

"Yes," Jennifer replied.

"Well, then," Brother Sebastian said as he stood up from his seat. "I want you to understand that, no matter what, we must always be honest about why we do things. We should never, ever allow ourselves to be fooled by ourselves. No matter what, we must be grounded in the truth. That's my lesson for today.

"So, two things: The first is to never lie to your parents. Once established, the trust between you and your parents is worth far more than any amount of gold. At the same time, it is always fragile and must be constantly earned. We're going to go up to the office, and I want you to call your mother. Tell her that Brother Sebastian is helping you check the location on the map, and that you'll get back to the hospital as soon as you can. I don't think she'll be surprised."

"Okay," Jennifer said.

"Second: If we move in the truth and the light, we'll go find where the creases cross."

CHAPTER

18

They made their way quickly to the river, with Jennifer jogging behind Brother Sebastian as he took long strides. They hurried through a scattering of buildings, passed by fields being tended by several men, and reached the forest where the canyon walls drew in closer to the river.

He knew the path through the woods and meadows that avoided the brambles and thickets that grew along the river's banks. They passed his small cabin. After a half-hour or so, she recognized the place where she had left her brother lying on the boulder. Several minutes later, they came to the large vertical cliff whose base reached the water, leaving no space for walking. She was surprised that they had moved so fast.

"How come the water's still high? I thought they turned it down on Sunday afternoon."

"You can never be sure," the monk replied. "They might need the water for irrigation or something. We'll be fine."

Jennifer watched Brother Sebastian as he kept his right hand on the side of the cliff, lifted the hem of his robe up with his left, and carefully stepped into the river.

His foot remained on top, startling Jennifer as he appeared to walk on top of the water's surface.

"This is probably the moment to tell the story of Jesus walking on water," he said, grinning as he looked back at Jennifer. "But the truth is that I moved several boulders over here to make a path for going around the cliff when the river is high. Watch my feet and put yours where I put mine."

He laughed.

Jennifer stepped as he did and found solid stone just beneath the surface. She laughed as she followed him quickly around the cliff's base.

"Okay, this is it," Brother Sebastian said as he stepped onto the riverbank. "Do you have the map?"

Jennifer jumped from the last boulder, reached into her daypack, and handed him the map.

"According to the creases," the monk said, "this is where Everett hid the gold. What's next?"

Before she could answer, a loud thumping sound came from the canyon ahead. It's noise increasing in volume, a helicopter suddenly zoomed overhead and then disappeared. The canyon quickly returned to silence.

Jennifer had shaded her eyes to watch the helicopter fly over and then turned back to Brother Sebastian. She hardly recognized the man.

The monk's calm, happy, relaxed face now held a grim expression. His eyes were focused, his brow furrowed, and his lips a thin, straight line. He turned to look up and down the land on which they stood and then called to her.

"Come with me, now!"

He led her away from the imposing cliff and into a section of oak thickets along the edge of the pine trees. Looking closely, he selected the thickest and walked to the side away from the cliff. Kneeling to reach the bottom branches, he bent them to the side, creating an opening.

"We're going to have some visitors that we don't want to meet. Let's hide in here. I'll be on the side toward the men who are coming, and I need for you to be directly behind me as close as you can get. Once they're here, do not move."

Getting into the thicket was not easy for the big man. Bending, turning, gathering, and twisting the thin branches, he opened a hollow space that Jennifer thought would have been impossible. He held his robe, pushed aside branches, and cleared a spot big enough for two. Finally he sat cross-legged and motioned Jennifer to crawl in behind him.

Brother Sebastian undid his rope belt and spread his robe to his side, hiding Jennifer even more. He pulled back some of the bent branches and moved them closer, filling in the empty space. He bent others over them, creating a shield of leaves.

"Take some of the leaves and spread them over me," he said in a quiet voice.

She grabbed at the thick layer of oak leaves and pine needles around them, gathering as much of the debris as she could, and spread them over the monk's robe. Then she took off her cap and moved closer to him, pushing her knees into the robe behind his arms and pulling branches closer to her as he had done. She tossed some leaves into her hair and pressed against his back.

Covered by the leaf clutter, the rustic brown cloth disappeared into the forest floor. The monk pulled the hood over his head, slipped his hands and arms into his sleeves, and sat motionless.

"Okay," he said calmly, "now we wait."

It was a perfect disguise. Viewed from the front, they appeared only as a denser blot of leaves within the thicket, no different from a hundred other blots in the forest.

Jennifer felt her heart beating and worried that it was loud enough to be heard. She had no idea why they had suddenly hidden themselves, but she assumed it had something to do with the helicopter. How Brother Sebastian reacted, though, was surprising. Did he recognize the helicopter? Did he know who owned it or where it was from? Why hide from it?

She had her answers a few minutes later as a small raft rounded a bend in the river and hit the bank not more than fifty feet from where they sat. Four men slid off the tubes, pulled the raft out of the water, and then gathered around to look at a piece of paper. She was surprised at how little sound they made.

She leaned closer to Brother Sebastian, trying to melt into his robe, but could not keep herself from peering around his shoulder.

Why do bad guys always wear black, she wondered. The men wore black caps, black T-shirts, black multi-pocketed pants, and black boots. Even their sunglasses were black.

The men unloaded two duffel bags, unzipped them, and assembled three metal detectors. Then three of them systematically moved across the area, sweeping the detector wands back and forth in front of them, moving from the river to the forest. The fourth man visually searched the forest, moving deep enough to touch the sandstone walls. He looked closely at the big trees, examined the open areas of the walls behind the trees, and ran his hands into any cracks he found in the rock.

Jennifer's heart pumped faster as the three men searched closer and closer to where she and Brother Sebastian were hidden. She pressed herself even closer to the monk, but he never flinched. At one point, she thought he had stopped breathing.

The men searched up to the thicket, swung around, and then moved back toward the river.

Not one of the detectors made so much as a single beep.

Continuing around the bank, the men finished the area in front of the trees. Then they moved closer to the tall sandstone cliff.

The cliff was massive, rooted deep in the earth and shooting straight up hundreds of feet. It was deep, projecting from the canyon walls at least a hundred feet into the canyon, ending in the shallows of the riverbed. There were swirls and notches and water trails in its pale-yellow surface and a grayish cap of rounded chalk on top.

Along the bottom was a considerable slope of rough rock—boulders, big mounds of rubble and dirt, collapsed slivers from the cliff that had fallen some eons before. The erosion had created a thick, jumbled apron of rocky confusion that spread out several yards deep.

At a point in the wall above the apron was a portion of the cliff that had split from the surface, a thick slab of sandstone now leaning outward, fifteen feet or so above the rock pile below it.

The men with the metal detectors moved onto the rock apron. Their paths were no longer orderly; they wandered in and out, up and down, around one boulder and back against another, always swinging the detector wands in front of them.

The fourth man moved back to the river and watched them, glancing closely at the paper in his hand, gazing upward and around the rim, shaking his head as his face displayed a look of disappointment.

The men found nothing.

They disassembled the detectors, put them back into the bags, loaded up the raft, and pushed off back into the water.

They paddled themselves down the river and out of sight.

CHAPTER

"They couldn't land the helicopter here," Brother Sebastian said. "It's declared a Wild and Scenic River along here, meaning that no mechanized vehicles are allowed below the rim of the canyon. I'm sure that whoever sent them didn't want someone's complaint to the river rangers to reveal that the team was here, so they probably were let out upstream at the junction of the Rio Cebolla and used a compressed air cartridge to inflate the raft. They may go all the way out now or they may hide along the canyon and go out after dark."

He and Jennifer waited five minutes before they moved. Once out of the thicket, they walked to the rubble next to the cliff, found a good rock, and sat down.

Jennifer had given up. Mogi was going to have live with a mystery that he could not solve. The people with the metal detectors had done far better than she and Sebastian could have done, and they had made the conclusion crystal clear: no gold.

"They wouldn't have hurt us, would they?" Jennifer asked. "I mean, if they had found us, they wouldn't shoot us or anything, right?"

Brother Sebastian considered her question. "I can't know what they would have done, but they weren't here for us, so I don't think they would have bothered us unless we tried to interfere with their prospecting. That's why I decided we should just sit and watch."

"But you knew they were coming when you saw the helicopter. How did you know they were coming and what they were going to do? How did you know how long we had?"

The monk's eyes became tinged with sadness. "I used to be one of those guys," he said.

"You used to be one of them? What, a gangster? A soldier?"

"When I was in high school, I thought the military was everything that I ever wanted," the monk said quietly. "I went to college, did the four-year ROTC program, joined up regular army, went to Special Forces training, and learned everything about how to wage war, how to blow things up, how to kill people.

"After a couple of tours in the Persian Gulf, I left the military and became one of these guys—a soldier for hire. Personal security details, special operations in sensitive countries, protection services for wealthy people. Men like these are not hard to find. Lots of ex-military like to play James Bond. It paid well, but the more I did it, the less I liked it. I finally faced the fact that I hated my life and that I hated me. So, I got out."

"And became a monk?" Jennifer asked, looking at his face.

"Oh, it wasn't that straight a path. My life took several turns before God brought me to my knees. Once on my knees, though, I never wanted to get up again."

It was noon, and Jennifer felt pressure to return to the hospital. Mogi's surgery was likely finished, so there was nothing to do but wait. It weighed on her that she had not been there for him but, given that he was the cause, it didn't weigh too much.

It also seemed of no value to stay at the area of the crossing creases: If there had been any gold buried along the river, certainly in the quantity of a hundred and fifty pounds, the metal detectors would have found it.

Good or bad, she felt that she should tell her brother as soon as possible. He had asked her to investigate, and she had done so; she'd held up her end of the commitment. He could have done no better. It would be deflating to him though, a hard disappointment.

Brother Sebastian seemed in no hurry to leave. Of course, he was home no matter what part of the canyon he was in, so Jennifer was not surprised when he stood on the riverbank and slowly rotated, seemingly spending time on every object that appeared in his sight.

But it was time to quit.

"Thank you," she said, walking over next to him, looking up. "I'm sorry I wasted your time."

"You're welcome," he said. "But whether it was a waste of time or not, I believe, is still to be determined."

"You can't think the gold is still here. We looked everywhere."

"Actually, we hardly looked at all. It was the men with the metal detectors who looked; we just accepted their conclusion. They didn't find it, so we assume it's not here."

Jennifer was confused. "Well, yeah. We could never have looked as well as they did, so I guess we were lucky they came along."

Sebastian smiled. "Me, too. Think of it—what were we going to do when we first came? We couldn't dig because we had no shovel. We couldn't turn over rocks because every rock of any real size is stuck well in the ground. It would have done us no good to search under any trees or around any of the vegetation because most of what we see didn't exist a hundred and thirty years ago.

"Doesn't it seem remarkable that for all we could not do—but wanted to do—there appeared three metal detectors out of nowhere to do it for us? Doesn't it, in fact, seem miraculous?"

Jennifer was thinking that the monk had been getting too much into the Communion wine. "Uh, well, I think we're lucky, but I'm not sure anything was miraculous."

"Well, even if we only call it lucky, doesn't it seem like an overwhelming amount of luck?"

"Is this a lesson or something? I should be getting back."

Brother Sebastian laughed. "Well, if it's a lesson, it's one for both of us. Forgive me for kind of being a 'professional' in this business, but having something drop out of the sky, like three metal detectors and men to do the search for us, should make us stand up and pay attention. That's what I've been doing, and I believe I've found something. . . ."

"What? You found something? I've been watching you—you haven't found anything."

"I found a question."

Jennifer felt like she was being played. Nice guy or not, if you've got something to say, say it.

"What? Just tell me!"

"Okay," Brother Sebastian said. "Forgive me for enjoying the moment. The question is, Was there any place the metal detectors did not look that could possibly have been a place that Everett Cossey used?"

"No," Jennifer said. "We watched them go over every piece of this riverbank."

"I agree. But consider this: They limited themselves to two dimensions—the ground and the rocks in the ground. They assumed that what they were looking for was buried. But we can raise our eyes and see in three dimensions, and I see one place that they did not look because it's not part of the riverbank. It is above it."

He took her by the shoulders, turned her body toward the cliff, and pointed to the slab of broken sandstone.

"But that's too high. Everett Cossey would never have been able to get up there. He would have needed a ladder or a. . . .

"Oh my God! The rope!"

CHAPTER

20

Jennifer's mother was not happy, and she let her daughter know it. Even with the phone call from the monastery, the whole adventure was based on deception.

"Yes, ma'am," Jennifer answered several times in their conversation.

Mogi listened. He wasn't the target of the reprimand, but he knew, as his mother well knew, that he was the major reason for the escapade. If Jennifer was in trouble, it was because he had put her up to it.

Physically, he was in good shape. The surgery was straightforward and had gone well. The anesthesia was local, so only his lower leg had been put to sleep. His ligament was repaired, and the ragged cut from the rock's edge was trimmed up and stitched. He was done in less than an hour.

He was not, however, in good shape mentally. It was 3 o'clock in the afternoon before Jennifer returned. That meant they had searched for a long time. That meant there was no gold.

No gold. No clever mark on the map. No Mogi miracle.

He felt better when Jennifer was finally standing next to his bed, but he knew he still had a lot of apologizing to do for sending her on yet another wild goose chase. And she had lied to their mother to do it. She looked at him with a humble expression, a proper I-accept-the-chewing-out-by-my-mother-because-I-earned-it expression.

Then she pulled over a wheeled table, reached into her pocket, and scattered a handful of dirty coins across the table's surface. And burst out laughing.

"Brother Sebastian and I decided I should take a few. I just had to show you what we found. And there's a *lot* more than this."

Mogi could hardly stay still on the hospital bed. He was grinning, laughing, pumping his fist, waving his arms, and singing a fight song. Their mother looked highly suspicious but still joined in their celebration.

Using the sink in the room and a towel over the drain, Jennifer cleaned up the handful of coins well enough for them to read the lettering and the dates on most of them. They were all American coins; most were gold, but several were silver. The dates ranged from 1855 to 1878.

"Wow" became Mogi's favorite word as he, Jennifer, and Mrs. Franklin examined the coins. He was soon using his iPad to record their face values and dates in a spreadsheet.

"Now what do we do?" Jennifer asked as her brother was clicking away.

"Oh, I have the answer to that one," their mother said. "We are first going to sit here and wait until they release your brother. Then we are going to get something to eat. Then we are going back to Ghost Ranch, where you, young man, are going to sit on the porch with your foot elevated for the rest of the day, and you, young lady, are going to sit there with him.

"I don't care if you did find bucketloads of valuable coins; they will wait. You will just sit and have a nice, quiet conversation about the fact that your adventures are driving your parents to an early grave. That being so, you will patiently give your mother one nice, quiet evening to finish preparing for her class. Understood?"

Yes, ma'am. Message received, loud and clear.

*　　*　　*

The abbot of the monastery visited the Franklins at Ghost Ranch that evening. Having suddenly been given piles of coins that weighed more than he did, he thought a personal visit was the least he could do. He was overwhelmed by the turn of events and thanked the family many times.

He was thankful, he emphasized, but maintained a steadfast attitude that money was nothing to be overwhelmed with. He was not a man devoted to money in any sense of the word, and he was more impressed with a five-dollar donation from someone who had little than a million-dollar donation from someone who had much.

But never having been faced with such a large donation, the idea that a few million dollars in gold and silver coins were now being sorted and recorded by a band of giddy monks back at the monastery left him somewhat stunned.

In the end, all he could do was listen as Jennifer recounted the happenings from the afternoon.

*　　*　　*

They needed a ladder.

After telling Jennifer his idea about the hiding place, Brother Sebastian excused himself, stepped around the skyscraper-sized cliff, and ran back to his cabin. When he returned, Jennifer was surprised that he had brought only a square-ish canvas bag.

Inside was an amazingly compact collapsible ladder.

"There are many piñon trees on the property," he explained. "I use the ladder to get piñon nuts whenever the trees produce."

Fully extended, the ladder was long enough to allow the tall monk to scramble the last two feet into the crack behind the angled slab of sandstone. It took only a minute before his grinning face appeared over the edge.

After that, it was a game of passing the empty ladder bag up to him, filling it with loose coins, and dropping it down to Jennifer, who had swept off an area on the bank to hold the growing stockpile of coins.

The bags holding the bank's money had long since dissolved, and it took considerable effort for Brother Sebastian to scrape through the foot of leaves, pine needles, dirt, bird poop, squirrel poop, mouse poop, and other substances that had formed thick patches of muck within and around the coins.

Once he was satisfied that he'd found all of the coins, the two of them brought the first load to the afternoon chant session that he had missed. Jennifer was sent on to the hospital while Brother Sebastian was given a stern word about putting money before spiritual growth.

Brother Sebastian humbly accepted his rebuke and then led a crowd of monks back for the rest of the coins. There were enough men and cloth sacks to require only one additional trip.

Once they were all bagged up and brought back to the monastery, the coins were dumped on a long table in the dining room. Pots of hot water, toothbrushes, and scrubbing cloths were brought in, and the brothers were soon crowding around to clean away a hundred and thirty years of accumulated dirt and grime.

It was obvious that the weight of the strongbox was an approximation, and the legend that all the coins were gold was not true. As the monks sorted the coins, they found that the strongbox had held plenty of ordinary currency—gold pieces in $20, $10, $5, and $3 denominations, plus a bucket full of Morgan silver dollars.

Sheila Winters had used the measure of a hundred fifty pounds of gold to judge the treasure's worth. With the lower denominations and some coins being silver, her estimate was too high. Judging by the current prices they had found on the internet, the coins were worth about $2 million.

CHAPTER

21

Tuesday was an uneasy day for Mogi. Yes, the monastery now had money to hire lawyers that could sue whatever entity ended up building the plant, but it still meant years of fighting in court. It seemed to him that the best way for everything to work out was for the monastery to buy the land instead of Sheila Winters, but with only $2 million, it couldn't be done. It felt like a third of a victory.

"What do you want?" Jennifer asked him. "Finding the gold was the idea, and you did that. Quit being so unreasonable. Isn't one miracle enough? The monks are not dumb people—they'll figure out a way to manage."

Mogi sat on an overturned bucket in the garden, and Jennifer sat a few feet away on her own bucket. His booted leg stuck out at an awkward angle to allow him to grab the stalk of an onion, give it a wiggle, and pull the bulb out of the ground. The afternoon rains had made the onions grow quickly, and each bulb in the row had almost pushed itself out of the ground, making the job easier.

He rubbed the dirt off the bulbs and placed them into a wide basket that sat along the row. After he had pulled those within reach, he raised himself up, moved the bucket and basket a few feet down the row, and settled down for another bunch.

Yes, he was being unreasonable. He and Jennifer and Brother Sebastian had done far more than anyone could have imagined. It would just be so nice if the monastery could trump Sheila Winters' offer. It would have made everything simpler, faster, and more satisfying.

But it wasn't going to happen. The abbot had said that the meeting to finalize the sale of the property was scheduled for ten o'clock on Wednesday, at the realty office in Chama.

That was tomorrow.

"Hey, pard. You up for a break?"

It was Ted, and Mogi was more than ready for a break. He left his bucket and basket of onions with Jennifer, and the two slowly made their way up to the ranch museum. A soft drink machine was tucked into the corner of the porch.

"Let me buy," Mogi said, pulling a handful of coins from his pocket. "I owe you a lot for the last three weeks."

Mogi sorted through the change, but before he could put the four quarters into the machine, Ted asked to see them.

"I always check quarters," he said as he fingered them. "I'm trying to get all the states. It doesn't make them worth any more, but I think having the whole collection would be fun."

When Ted handed the quarters back, Mogi slid the first quarter into the slot, hesitated, slid the second quarter in, and hesitated again. It was almost ten seconds before he slid in the other two.

Then, to Ted's surprise, Mogi leaned forward and banged his head on the machine. Once, twice, at least three times.

* * *

It was 9:55 on Wednesday morning in the real estate agent's office. The current owner of the property, Raymond Archuleta, was there, as were the agent, a bank representative, Sheila Winters, and her two lawyers. They were surprised when the monastery's leader came through the door.

The abbot was apologetic about showing up uninvited. He spoke gently, telling the group that he and Raymond were long-time friends and that he wanted to assure everyone that the monastery would be the best neighbor possible under the circumstances. Sheila Winters appeared uncomfortable and seemed about to speak up.

But then the abbot suggested that they pray for this time of great change. So he led a prayer.

For the future of the land.

For the people involved in the decision.

For the benefit of the surrounding ranches.

For the benefit of all the animals that lived on the land, as well as the fish that swam in the river and the birds that nested in the trees.

For the visitors that came to the monastery.

For each and every brother who lived at the monastery. And he listed them by name.

He was about to start praying for all the politicians who governed the land when there was a screech of tires, the slamming of a car door, and commotion on the sidewalk.

The door to the room jerked open and Mogi Franklin stumped in, followed by his mother.

The abbot said a quick "amen."

Still sweating from moving as fast as his ankle boot allowed him, Mogi took a seat next to his mother in chairs set away from the table. He removed a piece of paper from his pocket, tore off a corner, wrote a number on it, folded it, and passed it to the abbot.

The abbot held it under the table, unfolded it, and read the number.

His eyes grew large.

Taking a deep breath, he spoke.

"I am usually not one to hold on legalities," he said, looking around at the bewildered group. "But technically, the ten-day waiting period isn't over until the end of today. With that in mind, I must tell you that our monastic community has received an anonymous donation that will allow us to buy the property, to be paid in full immediately, if Raymond sees fit to reconsider his original offer to us."

Sheila Winters went through the roof. She and her lawyers immediately started threatening lawsuits, pointing fingers at the abbot, at Mogi, at the real estate agent.

Raymond Archuleta, however, just smiled.

CHAPTER

22

"**E**verything loaded?" Jennifer asked.

"Yup. We just need to say good-bye to everyone." Mogi sat down next to his sister on the porch swing of their casita. He propped his walking boot against the bare wood railing.

"I'm going to miss those onions," he said.

Jennifer laughed. "Well, I won't miss cleaning all those pots and pans. We need to come back someday though so I can go on one of those horseback rides you got to do."

He laughed. "We also need to stop at the library so I can get another copy of the research paper. I've got the map that Brother Sebastian marked up, but I want everything else, too."

"So, are you going to make me wait longer, or do I have to accidently bump your foot?"

Mogi looked surprised. "I figured it was perfectly obvious, so I wasn't sure I had anything to tell."

"Well, it's not that obvious, and I wasn't there at the end, so tell me the whole story."

Mogi smiled.

"It was Ted asking to look at my quarters when I was buying him a soft drink from the machine," he said. "A $20 gold piece in 1872, which weighed about one ounce, was worth $20 because gold was $20 an ounce. In today's money, the coin would be worth about sixty times more because gold is now about $1,200 an ounce. But what I had missed was that a $20 gold piece made in 1872 is worth a whole lot more than its weight in gold—to a coin collector.

"So, I needed a number for what all the coins from the robbery would be worth if they were sold not by weight or face value, but as individual rare coins. You were busy, so I got Mom to take me to the monastery. They had created a database of the coins and their dates, so I downloaded the data to my iPad. The monastery's internet time doesn't come up till night, so Mom and I went to Bode's General Store where they have WiFi.

"Just a quick look at eBay prices showed that some of the coins might be worth hundreds or thousands each, but each coin has to be professionally examined to know the exact amount. I found a website that offered to answer questions, so I emailed them a general idea of what we had—the number and variety of coins and the story behind them—and asked for help in determining a reasonable guess at their worth. But I didn't get an answer before they closed, so we had to go back on Wednesday morning.

"By the time we got back there, I only had an hour to determine some sort of value for all the coins. Thankfully, there was an email with a phone number, so I talked with this really enthusiastic coin collector in New York. It turns out that really serious coin collectors not only keep up with what coins exist in the world today and who has them, but they keep a list of instances in which coins have been lost—like coins lost in shipwrecks, stolen mail, train explosions, robberies, house fires. And guess what?"

"I give up."

"The Cossey robbery of 1882 has always been on their radar! The guy on the phone was crazy excited when I told him it had been found, like a kid on Christmas morning. But he couldn't give me a price on the collection because each coin still has to be evaluated. He sent me to a website of a coin magazine. He pointed out one particular article that I should read.

"Now, tell me we aren't lucky. In 1993, some guy started a research project on the Cossey robbery, tracking down what kinds of coins were likely to have been in the strongbox, where they came from, and in which mint they were made. From that information, he made guesses at what the worth might be. And you know what?"

"It was a lot?"

"Not only was it a lot for the coins, but he guessed that if the stash were ever found, coin collectors all over the world would compete for a chance to own *all* of them, rather than buying them individually, because of their historical value. He guessed at what a collector might pay in that case—$7 million! That's the number I gave to the abbot."

"So that's more than what Sheila Winters was about to pay for the land."

"Yup."

"Wow," Jennifer said. "That's a lot of money."

She was quiet for a few moments and then shook her head. "You did it again. Almost."

"What do you mean 'almost'?" Mogi asked.

Jennifer stood up, reached into her pocket, and took out two Morgan silver dollars. She sat down and handed him one.

"I kept these, so the monastery's collection is short by two coins," she said with a smile. "I figured we needed some souvenirs."

Mogi smiled, gave his sister a kiss on the cheek, and quietly slid the coin into his pocket. He leaned back, using his good foot to push the swing into a regular rhythm.

"Wait a minute," Jennifer said, quickly turning to him. "What about the guy who was drowned, stabbed, and shot? Did you figure out what happened?"

Mogi thought for a moment and replied, "Kind of. I don't know for sure, but Sheila Winters gave me a hint. Remember when I told you about the trail ride when she threw a rock at the horse? I told you about her eyes looking so evil? She was absolutely enraged. I bet she could have pushed that horse over the edge of the cliff with no guilt at all.

"I figure that's what happened with Orin Cossey. I bet he hadn't told Everett that he was planning to kill Tom and then plant the map on him. Orin probably knocked him over the head with a rock and drowned him and was waiting for Everett to show up with the gold and the boat.

"But when Everett doesn't show up, doesn't show up, doesn't show up, Orin finally loses it. He goes into a rage because his little brother has botched the one thing he had to do, and he takes it out on poor Tom's body, shooting him and stabbing him with his knife. All he could think about was losing all that money.

"Afterward, Orin rides away, taking the two horses and leaving his brother. Even if Everett had made it out of the canyon, he would have found himself abandoned. And God only knows what happened to the fourth guy."

Jennifer nodded. Sounded like Orin to her.

They sat quietly, knowing that they should get up and say their good-byes and thank yous and find their mom and start down the road, but they were reluctant to do so. The sky was clear, a light breeze made it cool in the shade, and the morning scents of the pasture, garden, and orchard were strong.

"Ah, well," Jennifer said. She stood and stepped onto the sidewalk. Her brother followed.

ABOUT THE AUTHOR

Don Willerton was raised in a small oil boomtown in the Panhandle of Texas, becoming familiar through family vacations with the northern New Mexico area where he now makes his home.

After earning a degree in physics from Midwestern State University in Texas and a master's in computer science and electrical engineering from the University of New Mexico, he worked for Los Alamos National Laboratory for almost three decades.

During his career there, Willerton was a supercomputer programmer for a number of years and a manager after that for "way too long," and also worked on information policy and cybersecurity.

He finds focusing on only one thing very difficult among such varied interests as home building, climbing Colorado's tallest peaks, and rafting the rivers of the Southwest (including the Colorado through Grand Canyon). Willerton also has owned a handyman business for a number of years, rebuilt old cars, and made furniture in his woodshop.

He is a wanderer in both mind and body, fascinated with history and its landscape, varied peoples and their cultures, good mysteries, secrets, and seeking out treasure. Most of all, he loves the outdoors and the places he finds in the Southwest where spirits live and ghosts dance. Weaving it all together to share with readers has been the driving force of Willerton's writing over the past twenty years.

River of Gold is the final book in the nine-book Mogi Franklin series of Southwest-based mysteries for middle-grade boys and girls.